Two Girls Who Danced With The Demon of Darkness

J. Wayne Frye

This book is written in Canadian English

Two Girls Who Danced
With the Demon of Darkness

About the Author (Wayne Frye)

Wayne Frye's *Aaron Adams* mysteries, *Chablis Louise Chavez* thrillers, *Girl* books and *Lynton* adventures titillate the brains of those who enjoy tantalizing tales of mystery. His sports book, *How Hockey Saved a Jew from the Holocaust* is required reading in many schools. Growing up in the small USA town of Asheboro, North Carolina, he wrote his first novel at 15, but waited over twenty years before submitting it to a publisher. His life, like the heroes he writes about, has been filled with adventure and excitement. He has been a college hockey coach, professor, and at one time, the youngest university president in the USA. Called a marketing genius by the *Los Angeles Times*, he has been a promotional consultant to hockey teams and motion picture companies, and he has been cited for his work with inner-city youth in Los Angeles. A proud Canadian, he lives in Nanaimo, British Columbia on Vancouver Island.

Some of the 80 Books by J. Wayne Frye

The author

White Meteors and the Ghost of Sue Ann McGee
Hockey Mania and the Mystery of Nancy Running Elk
Something Evil in the Darkness at Hopkins House
How Hockey Saved a Jew From the Holocaust
The Girl Who Stirred up the Whirlwind
The Girl Who Motivated Murder Most Foul
The Girl Who Said Goodbye for the Last Time
Fall from Apocalypse + Armageddon Now
Worth Part 1: Like a Comet in the Midnight Sky
Worth Part 2: The Night of Thunder Road
Worth Part 3: Moonshine and Ghosts
Worth Frye's Ghost: A Haunting Experience
The Return of Worth Frye's Ghost
When Jesus Came to Jersey as the Son of Thunder
When Jesus Came to Canada to Lead an Indigenous Rebellion
When Jesus Came to the Black Hills to do the Ghost Dance
When Jesus Came to Ladysmith to Battle the Angele of Death
Lynton Curls Her Hair   *   *Lynton Walks on Water*
Lynton and the Vampire at Tagaytay Manor
Lynton Buys a Cell-Phone and Hears the Voice of Doom
Lynton Viñas and Beowulf Perez in the Taal Inferno
Lynton and the Ghosts at the Mansion on Balete Drive
Lynton Viñas: Shadow in Darkness   *Lynton's South African Adventure*
Lynton and the Stellenbosch   * *Lynton and the Cape Town Ghost*
Lynton, the Karoo Vampire and the Jewels of Omar Bin Abi
Lynton and the Haunting of the HMS Wind Dancer
Lynton and the Ladysmith Phantom
Chablis and Lynton in the Room of Doom
Chablis: Avenging Angel for the Forgotten in the City of Lost Hope
The Girl With the Million Dollar Smile: The Lynton Viñas Story
The Terror

In 2012, Wayne Frye introduced the world to the beautiful, vivacious Scandinavian fireball, Jasmine Alexander, who met his renowned famous private eye, Aaron Adams, in Stockholm, Sweden; where she became a target for a deadly assassin known as the *Whirlwind*. She was indeed *The Girl Who Stirred up the Whirlwind*, but she also stirred up Aaron Adams. Their May-December titillating romance blossomed into a torrid love affair that led them into the pits of desperation as they barely avoided death at the hands of the *Whirlwind*.

She left Aaron out of fear that as long as he was with her he was also a target for assassination by C.I.A. agents bent on eliminating her as a threat to expose an incredibly wicked and sinister 1986 U.S. government undercover operation. Now in Morocco, she is combating a perverse attempt to wrap mankind in the most insidious wickedness imaginable. In the process, she meets famed demon hunter, Lynton Viñas, and together they vigorously fight an evil that goes beyond anything the world has faced before. This is an evil seemingly conjured up from the deepest recesses of hell, and a determined demon of darkness will attempt to trap Jasmine Alexander and Lynton Viñas in a lair of damnable, depraved, destructive wickedness.

<u>TO – Igbal Coddington</u>
<u>XXXXXXXXXXXXXX</u>
What a grand time we had in Sicklerville,
New Jersey as young Ph.D.'s just finding our way
in a world filled with excitement!

Copyright 2025
by
J. Wayne Frye

Catalogue Number: 20126196111

ISBN: 978-1-928183-73-0

Fireside Books – A Division of Peninsula Publishing

Two Girls Who Danced
With the Demon of Darkness
TABLE OF CONTENTS

Prologue
Ticket to Dance with the Demon of Darkness....5
Chapter 1
Glistened in the Darkness of Misery…………...13
Chapter 2
Wings of Angels or Wings of Demons…..……25
Chapter 3
The Fingers of Fate………………………..41
Chapter 4
Uneasiness Gripped Them……………………..53
Chapter 5
Challenge of Monumental Proportions………...73
Chapter 6
Evil of the Foulest Kind………………………..99
Chapter 7
Foster Fear…………………………………… 117
Chapter 8
What I Saw••••••••••••••••••••••••••••••••....129
Chapter 9
Face-to-Face with the Demon of Darkness…...139
Chapter 10
That Damn Phone…………………………..145
Chapter 11
There is Evil Afoot Here...………………161
Chapter 12
Reach Its Zenith in the Old Quarter…………..167
Chapter 13
I Guess I am Doomed…………………………177
Epilogue
Nick Beale Had Just Found That Out…………189

**Two Girls Who Danced
With the Demon of Darkness**

**Two Girls Who Danced
With the Demon of Darkness**

<u>PROLOGUE</u>
Ticket to Dance with the Demon of Darkness

*Gliding gracefully across the floor,
Just come through my demonic door.
Does anyone have the courage to question hell?
If so, how long do you have to live to tell?*

The beautiful, provocative Jasmine Alexander did not believe in ghosts or demons and neither did the aging adventurer and erstwhile private eye, Aaron Adams, who had been her lover so many years ago back in Stockholm, Sweden. But neither the sturdy scepticism of one, nor the outright scoffing of the other was a shield against the horror that fell upon Jasmine in Morocco, the horror forgotten by many for so many years, a screaming fear that was viciously, diabolically and monstrously resurrected from the deepest pit of hell.

Jasmine had slipped out of Aaron Adams' life one night while he was sleeping, after the two of them had stirred up the infamous assassin known as the *Whirlwind*. At the time, Aaron was 62 and Jasmine was 26, but it was not the age difference that made her decide to leave him in the dark, early morning hours that faithful day. Rather, it was fear of a coming calamity perpetrated by the one nation that always was willing to go to any lengths in search of those who dared defy it. The United States government was after Jasmine Alexander, because she simply knew too much about an undercover CIA operation that had led to the assassination of Prime Minister Olaf Palme of Sweden in 1986. As long as Aaron Adams was with her, he, too, was a target. Therefore, her deep and abiding love for him made her decide to protect him the only way she knew how, by leaving. It had been over thirteen years, but now she needed him desperately.

What brought her out of the darkness of lonely, self-imposed exile in a North African enclave of anonymity is a story of horror that manifests itself in the spirit as much as in the ghostly apparitions of despair which haunt so many nightmares. But Jasmine was a resilient, determined woman who never bowed before the altar of fear. She would have to muster all her courage to survive the coming calamity.

Two Girls Who Danced
With the Demon of Darkness

How she was exposed to an abominable evil that was about to incubate and grow into a monstrous apparition of terror is a tale that goes back many years, when the horror first manifested itself. Dedicated men and women had investigated the evil over the years, but none had been able to corral and isolate it to protect people from harm. However, an admission this evil existed was often met with great scepticism and outright rejection.

Religion was the opiate of the masses and kept the majority of the world in bondage to the hope of pie in the sky in the sweet by-and-by, while the privileged classes enjoyed their pie now rather than later. So, those who fell for the after-life promises of gaining all they were denied in life were easy prey for the idea of demons and devils bounding about ready to do evil things. Yet, were all the musings of charlatans total fiction?

Jasmine Alexander had scoffed at the idea of demons and devils, because she was free of the manipulative structure of religion. However, that all dramatically changed one day at a bazaar in the Old City section of Casablanca, where she had gone after leaving Aaron to hide out from a world that was held in the iron grip of a country that had deemed her expendable for what she knew about the CIA sanctioned assassination of Olaf Palme back in 1986. Although only a very young little girl at the time, Jasmine Alexander had unwittingly come face-to-face with the deadly assassin, the *Whirlwind*, and had, at a later time in life, put the pieces of a complex puzzle together.

Two Girls Who Danced
With the Demon of Darkness

By doing so, she had become a target for assassination herself, and in desperation had embraced Aaron Adams as her saviour, only to fall in love and realize that the way to save him was to extricate herself from a relationship that also made him a target. (Although not germane to the story told here, for those wanting further clarification on the love affair between Aaron and Jasmine, it would be appropriate to read *The Girl Who Stirred up the Whirlwind*.)

That day in Old City, which was also where Jasmine lived in a one room flat above a rug merchant's shop, was the beginning of what would be a harrowing battle with the forces of darkness in a world where evil manifests itself daily through the promotion of greed as an enviable trait. The pathway of mankind for many generations had been hijacked and damned by those who professed fealty to the idea that humanity can best be served through a system of economic bondage. This was the modern world.

Walking into an Old Quarter shop, Jasmine turned to her left and noticed the proprietor, who was wearing a fez on his bald head, along with a traditional long flowing loosely-fitting caftan, as he stood slightly slumped over an oak counter. In the USA, Muslims are painted as dark, shifty-eyed, venal and threatening. How ridiculous thought Jasmine as she looked at the thin, jocular-looking man who greeted her with a toothless smile and a waving right hand. Jasmine, like most Europeans, because of their superior education system, was skilled at picking up languages, and she exchanged pleasantries with the old man in relatively fluent Arabic, which she had picked up since hiding out in Casablanca. Although she still dearly loved Aaron Adams, her insatiable appetite for sex had not precluded her from engaging in sexual trysts with Arabic men, who had also helped her learn the language. As she conversed with the old man, her eyes wandered to her right, where an ancient telephone sat on a curio cabinet.

For some reason, she felt compelled to examine it. Picking up the phone, she could feel warmth. It exuded a hotness that did not scorch, but did make one aware that there was an intense amount of heat being emitted from the phone.

How strange thought Jasmine, as she placed the telephone on the curio stand, turned and started to walk away. Then, she abruptly came to a halt and turned back to stare at it as if compelled to do so by some mysterious force. Standing there was a portly man of obvious European heritage pointing at the phone. She blinked her eyes and the man was gone, disappeared into thin air. Strange. Was he there or had she just imagined him?

Two Girls Who Danced
With the Demon of Darkness

She thought back on a book she had once read about a person who bought a telephone and used it to talk to people from the future, and she felt that she was actually staring at her future when she looked down at the telephone. But what of the past she thought? Was it really gone just because time moved on, or did it linger in another dimension just floating about, waiting to be resurrected by an inquiring mind? What of the bridge that links today with yesterday? What of the creatures that haunt the nightmares of the present but are rooted in the past? It was as if the phone was luring her into an unknown world that was menacing, mysterious and strange. Yet, she slowly moved toward the phone again as if in a trance, thinking about all the people who, over the years, had conversations on the phone about mundane and trivial things, about tragedies, about joyous events. It was so old fashioned that there was not even a dial on it, as early telephone companies had operators do the dialling for you. Then, she stood at that table completely mesmerized, wondering how many evil intentions had been manifested and shared over that phone. How much evil had been contemplated in various conversations?

Jasmine had to have the phone. There simply was no resistance left in her. She reached down, picked it up and walked toward the counter and the jocular toothless old man. Unknowingly, she was preparing to purchase her ticket to dance with the demon of darkness.

Two Girls Who Danced
With the Demon of Darkness

CHAPTER 1
Glistened in the Darkness of Misery

I am as far as the deepest sky between clouds,
And you are as far as the deepest root and wound,
And I am as far as a train distant from the station,
As far as a whistle you can't hear or remember.

In her bedroom that night, Jasmine sat staring at the phone. There was something hypnotic about its power to elicit awe from her. She was expecting one of her lovers whom she used for pleasure only. There was no emotional attachment to the young, virile man; although, he was a nice enough chap. Unlike the mundane American mass media characterizations of Muslim men, he was actually the typical well-educated modern Muslim man who was respectful, caring and extremely protective of women who refused to submit to the primacy of the male in just one of the absurdities in the many religions that people blindly followed in the belief doing so would get them a place in that grand paradise up in the sky after death.

Jasmine was simply unwilling to let herself get emotionally attached to any man, because she could not release herself from the intensity of the few months she had spent with the most wonderful man she had ever known. Aaron Adams was not really a great physical lover. His age and medical condition left him sorely wanting in that respect, although he did perform less strenuous forms of sex with great virtuoso. Yet, Jasmine, unlike many people, viewed sex as nothing more than a recreational activity. She was not in any way constrained by conventionality or religion. In Aaron, she had found more than physical attraction; although, for a 62 year old man, he wasn't bad looking and maintained a relatively decent physique. But none of that mattered, because in him she discovered the deep underpinnings of an emotional bond that stretched across time, place and space. She had an abiding attachment to a man who had stirred within her something she simply couldn't understand.

Still, as she reclined on the bed staring at the phone, she could not help but contemplate what he might think of her liaisons three or four times a week with men just for the pleasure of sex. Like him, she was not constrained by the conventions of a world where morality was defined by churches, synagogues, mosques, temples or self-serving corporate-controlled governments. She was a free-thinker who let no one force their interpretation of morality on her. She knew where real morality lay. It was not in the Bible, the Koran, the Torah or any other religious document. It was in the heart, and her heart was as pure as any that ever beat.

So far, she had not picked up the receiver on the phone, only gazed with bewilderment at the mouthpiece on the top of the narrow metal stem and the earpiece that hung in the cradle. She had always been fascinated by antiques. Aaron had jokingly told her once that was why she was attracted to him, because he certainly was a relic of the past. Still, she could not help but wonder why she had felt so compelled to buy this particular antique?

She reached over and very gently, with an almost emotional attachment, touched it with her right hand, in a nearly sensual fashion. Its heat was obvious, but it was not so hot that one felt the hand might be scorched. It was only an intense hotness that caused no pain, but rather consternation and curiosity.

Jasmine's tiny studio bedroom was rather lavishly furnished for the particular area of the Old City where she lived, which was actually called Old Medina. There was a stately old wooden fireplace mantle with a 1930's heater insert replacing the hearth. A thick wooden door to her right opened onto a back porch that was used for a private entrance above stairs to the teeming alley below. The muffled sounds of humanity parading through the ancient district could be faintly heard.

She glanced at the front door, which she had left unlatched at the top of outside stairs leading to a small porch. Light was beginning to fade as the sun slipped behind the ancient buildings to signal the close of another day in the Old City, as it had done for thousands of years.

Lying back on the bed, Jasmine looked at the clock. It was 7:30, and her lover, Arif, would walk through the door shortly and they would have frantic sex for a couple of hours. She expected no dating, no flowers or presents. All she sought from men was sex, but they all eventually became so enamoured and overwhelmed with her beauty, kindness, erotic sensuality and intellect that each one fell in love with her. It was never a conscious effort on her part. It just happened. It simply was the way things were. She gave them no encouragement or even hope that things might lead to more than a sexual relationship. Still, they persisted in pursuing that which was simply unattainable. She had been to the mountaintop of deep, abiding love with her beloved Aaron and she would never go there again with another man. Arif was no different than the many others.

She glanced over at the phone again. Still, she could not bring herself to lift the earpiece from the cradle. Something within seemed to be warning her it was not a good idea to place the earpiece next to her coal black, luxuriously radiant hair that cascaded over her shoulders and listen intently to a voice that shouldn't be there from what now seemed to be more than a mere candlestick telephone. There was just something about it that made her wonder why she felt so compelled to purchase it? She certainly didn't need it. It was functionally useless, anyway.

Jasmine was making her living by working in the rug shop below, cleaning the store and keeping books for the owner, who was also one of her lovers. As part of her pay, he allowed her to use the small, but comfortable one room apartment for accommodations. He was an older man, probably nearing 60 and a bit portly, but she had never been one to eschew lovers just because they happened to be less than attractive. She looked for the depth of character in a man, rather than physical attractiveness and the rug merchant, although married, was a man who had a sensitive nature. He loved his wife dearly, but like all men, feared the approaching tangle with the grim reaper with trepidation and dread that somehow he had not had enough sex in his life. After all, most men felt that they could never get enough sex. They simply failed to realize that no matter how much they got, it would never be enough. On the other hand, Jasmine could take it or leave it; although, she much preferred to take it, and as she always said, "sex is easy to get for a woman. You can get it on any street corner, but love has nothing to do with sex."

Two Girls Who Danced
With the Demon of Darkness

She had been in love with a woman in Stockholm, but that woman had been killed by the assassin, the *Whirlwind*. The sex with Rose was intense, but there was much more to their relationship than that. It was the first time in her life she was really in love, and just being in Rose's presence brought great solace to a life that had been filled with despair. Then, there was Aaron Adams, an older man whose libido had faded into nothing more than a memory. Still, just being in his arms, feeling his grizzled, calloused hands stroke her soft skin and melting into ecstasy as he fondled her mound of desire, gently probing its depths with his fingers as he suckled on her breasts, was like no sex she had ever experienced before or would ever experience again. She thought to herself that sex was more in the mind than the body. Of course, she was about to get her body ravaged by a virile young man who, like the rug merchant, was married. In fact, she preferred married men for sex partners, because it presented fewer complications in most cases. They, like she, were mostly looking for sex, so all the peripheral manifestations of the courting ritual were not necessary or needed as a prelude to pleasure.

The door slowly opened and there stood Arif smiling affectionately down at her. She whirled around to face him as he moved toward the bed. She gently lifted her dressing gown off her lithe, yet muscular body that was like a beacon guiding a lover to paradise between her spread legs where musky moisture was forming in anticipation of a

Two Girls Who Danced
With the Demon of Darkness

nimble, darting, probing tongue that would prime her for the pounding she craved from a man whose member was the piston that cranked her motor. Sex, for her, was nothing more than relaxation. It could include love, but that was not a necessity. Simple, unbridled passion was the premise.

Arif, frantically removing his clothes, dropped to his knees as her legs dangled over the side of the bed. He gently stroked her tight, muscular thighs as he dived into her gigantic mound of gratifying contentment that was offered so freely and willingly. She wrapped her legs around his neck, pulling his entire face into the sloppiness of paradise. He made gurgling sounds as he lapped up the flowing juices of delight that sent shivers through his body as his throbbing member dramatically rose to the occasion.

She released her grip, putting her legs high in the air and pulling them back to her chest, offering him the secondary hole that she knew he craved. She fondled her breasts as she lay back, moaning in anticipation of the ultimate in sexual penetration. Arif could not control his passion. He plunged into the wide opening and started furiously pounding her gorgeously generous ass that had an opening as wide as the Grand Canyon.

There was beauty in her dark eyes, reflecting the grandeur of a woman who was wanton and free. Her moaning began to sound like the resounding tempo of a Wagner concerto. She was not the gentle daisies that grow tall and pure upon the earth, reaching upwards in the sunshine. No, she was the rapturous, wild flower that grows free for all to enjoy. She, in that moment, was a true masterpiece of powerful femininity, naturally evolving from one masterpiece to the next, a perfect picture of time without hands or measure, but still always moving onward, more honest than any clock, because at that very moment time stood still. Her beauty and free spirit was an ever-present season. Yet, with her, one always felt the heat of summer, the heat of unbridled passion that rattled and shook the earth to its core.

Exploding like a volcano blowing its top Arif dumped a load of steaming hot joy juice deep within her cavity. He let out a satisfying long moan, as Jasmine, contracting her muscles to milk every last drop from his member, sighed with delight. She could sleep well now, having been to the Valhalla of sexual fulfillment.

Arif pulled his shrinking member out of her, and stood there exhausted. He crawled in bed beside her and as they both stared at the ceiling, he said, "You are the most extraordinary woman I have ever known."

Smiling as she glanced over at him, she replied, "I bet you say that to all the girls you plunge that monster into."

Laughing, he offered, with a sincere tone in his voice, "Not true my dear. Not true at all."

They cuddled in blissfulness for awhile, and then Arif got up, and as he was putting his clothes back on looked over at the phone she had bought. He stared at it for a long while, finally saying,

Two Girls Who Danced
With the Demon of Darkness

"That is a real old one. Last time I saw one that ancient, was when I watched an old Charlie Chan movie on television. Those things haven't been around since the 1930's, even here in Morocco. You can't use it, because it doesn't have a dial."

Standing up, still naked, Jasmine was not interested in what he said about her antique phone. She was now smiling in a tantalizingly mischievous way at Arif. She had no shame in her nakedness. In fact, she enjoyed being naked, enjoyed what her nakedness did to men. It was certainly having an effect on Arid. He stopped putting his clothes on as his member began to rise. He had just finished an episode of frantic, mind-blowing sex, but he was ready to go again.

Jasmine moved toward him with her puffy lips parted, showing her glistening white teeth. Their mouths met in a passionate kiss, while Arif let his pants drop to the floor around his ankles. He was breathing heavy with anticipation, because he knew what was about to happen.

Jasmine dropped to her knees and gobbled up his member in one giant gulp that made Arif let out a sigh of delight. He knew he was about to receive what he had received many times before, but each time she did it there was new magic in her technique. This time she used the swirling twist technique, moving her head in a swirling motion from side-to-side without un-gorging herself from his pole of delight. She kept twisting and twisting and twisting until he exploded again with the force of a bullet bursting forth from the barrel of a gun. This was something that gave Jasmine a sense of power, knowing that she had coaxed the elixir of life from a man's member into her warm mouth.

The two of them lay down for a few minutes until Arif looked at the clock and said he needed to get home. Jasmine smiled and said, "Goodnight, and remember I still have another hole that needs filling. It gets jealous if it gets neglected."

Exhausted, Arid said, "I am spent. No more please."

"Ah," replied Jasmine. "How cruel to neglect one of my gapping holes."

Shaking his head, Arif got up, put his pants on a second time resolved to not go another round. Jasmine spread her legs, and began to play with herself.

"I can't. I can't. I am exhausted," offered Arif.

Laughing, Jasmine said, "Killjoy."

With a look of determination, Arif gazed down at her and sighed. "I gotta go. I have to."

Still playing with herself, Jasmine parted her luscious lips and whispered as she motioned with her free hand. "I bet I can get it up one more time."

Arif stopped putting his shirt on, tossing it aside. He quickly removed his pants and looked down at his member, which was hanging sadly now. Jasmine rolled onto her side and motioned him over to the bedside. As he stood there, she eased it into her mouth and started sucking gently. It slowly came to life, and she rolled onto her back, spreading her legs. Arif eased into her honey pot and the blissfulness of coupling started again.

Being able to manipulate men was something Jasmine prided herself on, and well she should, because no one was ever able to eschew her erotic machinations. Poor old Arif left that night hardly able to walk down the stairs, so drained was he.

Jasmine, still lying on the bed naked, stared intensely over at the phone. What was it about that damn thing? What made it feel so hot to the touch? What was it that made it so intriguing to her? She couldn't figure out why she had to have it?

Longing is being wrapped up in desire, but it is broader than that. Jasmine saw in that phone an intense longing for the past, a lost experience, a pining for something that had been gone far too long. Desire was an itch that wants to be scratched, but longing was the ache accompanying a deep need that resides in the heart.

She took a long deep sigh and recited out loud a poem by Wadsworth from her youth:

> For oft, when on my couch I lie
> In vacant or in pensive **mood,**
> They flash upon that inward eye,
> Which is the bliss of solitude;
> And then my heart with pleasure fills,
> And dances with the daffodils.

She had to now confess suffering from a certain sickness for what had been lost that she long ago ardently and earnestly embraced. Sometimes, when no one saw her, she would pine alone for what she had years ago with Aaron. Her heart ached for the kind of love they shared, a kind of love that brightened each day. The kind of love that even in turmoil sparkled and glistened in the darkness of misery.

CHAPTER 2
Wings of Angels or Wings of Demons?

*Lynton is a beautiful woman
Who uses her lips for truth,
Her voice for kindness,
Her ears for compassion,
Her hands for charity
And her heart for love.*

By way of explanation to those not familiar with the famous Filipino demon hunter, Lynton Viñas, whose beauty and intelligence, along with her expertise in hunting demons is legendary in the Philippines, the USA, Canada and South Africa, let it suffice to say that it has been a privilege to scribe in print her extraordinary exploits that are often questioned for veracity by many, but I can categorically state herein that I have never had any reason to entertain doubts, despite being a doubter myself of the supernatural, of her sincerity and believability in recounting her exploits battling demons. There have been many eye witnesses to her exploits, and one of those eye witnesses is the famed private eye, Aaron Adams. It was his description of her to me that I used in my first book about her exploits. Looking at me in earnest, he said of her: "Her eyes are dark and alluring, dark as chocolate, dark as coffee, dark as the polished wood of a Chippendale credenza. They are set in a dark face, oval-shaped like a teardrop of passion. Her easy smile could stop a man's heart. Her lips are puffy and succulent, as if she had been eating sweet red berries. Her perky breasts are obviously soft, supple and pointed with twin peaks that remind the observer of magnificent snow capped mountains in the Alps. If she stands in a room, in a hallway, on the street, she is unmistakably the centre of attention. All eyes, even the eyes of women, are concentrating on her. However, do not misunderstand. She is not loud or vain, self-centered or self-absorbed and she never craves attention. We stare at a fire because it flickers, because it glows. The light in her is what catches our eyes, but what makes a person lean close to a fire has nothing to do with its brightness. What draws you to a fire is its warmth, and so it is with Lynton. Her real attraction is her warmth and sincerity."

Two Girls Who Danced
With the Demon of Darkness

How this woman, affectionately called the dynamic dynamo, wound up in Casablanca is remarkable in that it put her in the right place at the right time to meet Jasmine Alexander and join her in an adventure that would test their courage and devotion to justice. Lynton's sole purpose is, and always has been, to facilitate honesty and truth in a world where it is in short supply. She also knows the real and most hideous demons are not the supernatural ones. Rather, they are of the human kind.

She wound up in Casablanca after making a nostalgic trip to where her love once grew and blossomed in Cape Town, South Africa, generally declared by travel aficionados as the most beautiful city in the world. It was there over a three year period she attended graduate school in that magnificent city. While renewing old acquaintances on a nostalgic journey, she and the author of this book were enjoying a delightful interlude with old friend, Andiswa Solani, at their favourite restaurant, Stacked Diner, which was right below the famous Table Mountain, when Wayne Frye received an urgent message from his Los Angeles agent who said he needed to meet with a motion picture producer who was anxious to secure rights to all his Aaron Adams mysteries. He and Lynton had planned on going to Casablanca, and were looking forward to their trip there. Wayne encouraged her to make the trip to Casablanca alone, and enjoy herself. They already had reservations at the Casablanca White Butterfly

Two Girls Who Danced
With the Demon of Darkness

Hotel, which was in the Old City section of the metropolis. A day later, after arriving in Casablanca, Lynton was meandering through the Old City shops when she happened to venture into the same shop where Jasmine Alexander had become fascinated with the ancient telephone. It was there, where she was not doing a thing one day except leaning against a pillar looking at a table full of antiques that fate would step in. There, she was observed by Abi Muhammad, the proprietor, who stated later for publication, "She was doing nothing but holding the universe together with her nonchalantness and beauty."

It was at this time that Lynton dispassionately moved toward the counter, where displayed behind Abi Muhammad she noticed a huge movie poster from the film, *Casablanca*. There was something captivating about it.

She stood staring at it as Abi Mohammed said to her, "The Old City, Casablanca and Humphrey Bogart are irresistibly linked to my country. It is a romantic ideal that has lived on ever since the movie came out in 1942. Personally, I like Bogart better as Philip Marlow or Sam Spade in *The Big Sleep* and *The Maltese Falcon*. Now those two guys were the real prototypes for private eyes. Why I just had a lady in a few days ago who bought an old phone from the 1930's. It was actually used in the movie, *The Big Sleep*. I bought it when I was shopping for antiques in Los Angeles a few years ago. Found it in a really curious little antique shop down in Hollywood.

Two Girls Who Danced
With the Demon of Darkness

Lynton said, "I know the shop I bet. It was called Hollywood Curios down an alley off Santa Monica Boulevard in West Hollywood. Right?"

"That's it."

Smiling, Lynton said, "The shop had a lot of Ida Lupino memorabilia all around the place."

"Yeah," offered Abi Mohammed.

Lynton said, "The shop is gone now. One day I was in it looking at stuff, and a strange man, a Frenchmen – no, he said he was from Belgium, actually, but he had a thick French accent. He said something really strange to me."

With a look of astonishment, Abi Mohammad interjected, "I met the same man. He is the one who convinced me to buy the phone. He said, as he pointed at the phone in the shop, that is a portal to the past, and a conduit to the future. Be careful with it, because it has mystical powers. It should only be sold to a person of integrity and great courage. That is important."

Lynton, a startled look on her face, said with deep conviction in her manner, "I think it was the same man approached me. It was like he came out of nowhere, just appeared suddenly, standing beside me. He told me to be careful what you buy, because of my reputation, and many items carry with them danger, danger that only a person of my supernatural knowledge would understand."

Lynton continued, "I decided not to buy anything from there. I had a bad feeling about the place. Yet, I went back the next day, and the place had closed up. It was empty, completely empty."

**Two Girls Who Danced
With the Demon of Darkness**

Abi Mohammad took a long, drawn out breath. "I had the same feeling. Yet, I felt compelled to buy that phone. I don't know why. It sat in my shop for years with no interest until this beautiful woman came in a few days ago and seemed lured to it. I was actually reluctant to sell it to her."

*Original Lobby Card from movie Casablanca
that was behind the antique shop counter.*
©1942 and ©1970 Warner Brothers Pictures

Two Girls Who Danced
With the Demon of Darkness

Lynton, her intense curiosity aroused, asked Abi Mohammad to point where the antique phone had been displayed. He seemed hesitant as he, nervously, with shaking index finger, pointed to a far corner.

Lynton moved there and just stood for a few seconds, placing her hand on the table where the phone had been. Looking at Abu Mohammad she said, "The woman's name?"

"I don't think it would be ethical for me to give it out."

Lynton, for a reason she could not fathom, felt compelled to see that phone, but did not want to press the issue with the shop owner. Smiling at Abi Mohammad, she said, "I understand."

Now, one might logically ask why Lynton was so interested in the phone. It just so happened a few years before in the Philippines she had purchased a cell phone and started getting strange calls on it from someone who had died. Her husband, Wayne Frye wrote a best-selling book, *Lynton Buys a New Cell Phone and Hears the Voice of Doom*, about the episode. Ever since then, she had been interested in telephones. Perhaps drawn to them, expecting communication perhaps from a dead person. A bit childish she knew, but yet she could not abate the interest in them.

Feeling a great simpatico with Lynton, Abi Mohammad in a near whisper said, "You know, I think you are a sincere person. I see no reason why I shouldn't give you the lady's name."

Two Girls Who Danced
With the Demon of Darkness

He slowly moved to the left of the counter he was standing behind, bent down and removed a small file box. He pulled out a card and wrote Jasmine Alexander's name and address on a piece of paper.

Shocked that Jasmine Alexander was using her real name, Lynton was mortified with disbelief, because although she had never met the woman, she did know of her, because her husband, Wayne Frye, was author of the Aaron Adams mysteries, and it was he who had written *The Girl Who Stirred Up the Whirlwind*, which detailed the story of intrigue, mystery and U.S. government malfeasance in the assassination of Olaf Palme, Prime Minister of Sweden. She was about to meet Jasmine Alexander, and also become embroiled in a mystery that would try her soul.

It was in Casablanca that Lynton would remember *Rick's Café Americain*, a wonderful place that had been tastefully reproduced in Cape Town, South Africa, where she and her husband had dined often when they lived there. Now she was actually in Casablanca, where a modern version called *Rick's Cafe* was near the Old City Section. She was heading to meet Jasmine Alexander and get a look at the phone that for some unknown reason was seemingly luring her. She would not mention to Jasmine that she knew who she really was, because obviously she had left Stockholm to escape the long arm of the sinister USA and the nefarious C.I.A. which was every bit as pervasive as the old Gestapo during World War

Two Girls Who Danced
With the Demon of Darkness

II Germany in hunting down its adversaries. Perhaps she used her real name, because she thought doing so would throw off any pursuers, as they would assume she would never use her real name in hiding. Anyway, it had been 13 years now, so perhaps the C.I.A. had moved on to other heinously odious pursuits in its never-ending delusional beliefs that the entire world was out to destroy all that illusionary freedom Americans believed they had while living in the most repressive so-called democracy in the world.

The western idea of Morocco, and especially Casablanca, was eternally trapped in the World War II era and the idea promulgated by memories of Humphrey Bogart and Ingrid Bergman that seemed to promise it would remain so forever. Some even put it farther back with the mental and spiritual clock set to a time when Nomadic Berbers roamed the sands of the desert, but for Lynton that was a compliment, not a slur, as she found the old world charm soothing to her sense of nostalgia for simpler ways in simpler times.

It was winter in Casablanca, which was actually somewhat cool by African standards, as most of Morocco has a mild climate compared to the rest of the continent. In reality, Casablanca appeared far away from the world, and almost asleep; almost stuck in that long ago time when it was still like a little village in the middle of a primal sleep, nestled elegantly against the backdrop of the Mediterranean. It drowsed peacefully in solitude where news from the world hardly ever came to disturb its dreams, and it appeared infinitely content at least on the surface. Yet, the ancient old quarter of the city, renowned for perceived mystery, was bathed in intrigue and the reflections of times long past. The image of the Old City Section described, drawn, painted and photographed repeatedly by travelers, artists and architects became engraved in the collective imagination, especially through the movie, *Casablanca*. It was nurtured with the Oriental cultural repertory on Islam enhanced by the creation of a myth which had been promulgated by Hollywood. The myth was a system of communication, an enduring message of intrigue and romance. It was defined by the way in which it uttered this message, and not by the object of its message. It was chosen by history as interpreted in Hollywood. In this myth was the discourse that framed the Old City Section with certain enduring, almost mythological concepts.

The myth of the Old City developed around three concepts: gender, mystery and difference. The first was linked to the broader project of the feminization of the East as Moroccan women were the key symbols of cultural identity for Westerners who saw the belly dancers in Hollywood films and those exotic women became sexually idealized in the Western mind. An old Moroccan philosopher once said, "He who has never loved, never sought out the fragrance of a delicate flower and never quivered gazing at a Moroccan woman has never known what true beauty is."

Two Girls Who Danced
With the Demon of Darkness

Looking about while she strolled through the Old City in search of Jasmine Alexander's residence, as she was unable to use the GPS on her phone since there was no signal in the area she observed the Old City Quarter as a wise and dangerous mistress that exuded a climate of caress and torpor, mystery and intrigue, suggesting that it exerted a control over mind and body as its mystique engulfed you.

Popular literature that Lynton had read abounded with descriptions of Casablanca as a woman, often an excessively sensuous one that could wrap you in its arms and enthral you with its charms. Lynton's own disarming charms made her a perfect fit for Casablanca. They complimented each other, as like the city, she was strong-minded, strong-hearted, strong-souled, strong-bodied, as she effectively blended strong-beauty and strong-will in a kaleidoscope of grandeur.

The murmur of the distant waves against the white sand of the beach was as sweet to the ears as the rippling of the breeze in the palm trees of an oasis! Seductive and easy-going, Casablanca could be loved for the deep purity of her sky, the radiant splendour of her turquoise sea, her mysterious smells, the warm breath in which she wrapped her visitors like a long caress.

Casablanca was like a magnificent female body, supple-hipped and full-breasted, a body which could be revealed in all its magnificence through the judicious influence of form to harmonize natural topography and human geometry into a feeling, a feeling of being in consonance with nature.

Hand in hand with its gendered sensuality, the Old City evoked mystery. It represented the attractions of unknown dangers and marked the difference between cultures and even formed for some observers an inspiring contrast to the modernity of the Occidental as one could push open a door to enter into a magic land.

Even when the observer did not romanticize about the Old City Section, he or she attributed grand elements of mystery and unfamiliarity to it as one could not help but be overwhelmed by the dramatic transition from culture to culture as one took in the discreetly contemplative aged quarters of Old City with its bazaar-laden streets that had mysterious winding stairways leading to silent climbs upward to hidden shops and homes. The transition was rapid and the change of place complete as Lynton recognized the more beautiful sides of the Arab and Berber people on the teeming streets, embracing the simple observation of people capable of comprehending the grandeur of Moroccan humanity, those sides that make a contrast with the sad example that was promoted in movies and by self-serving politicians in the western world. Descriptions and lurid commentaries on the city perpetuated the myth that restricted the city and remade its people according to favourite allegorical paradigms, effectively freezing the Old City Section in a mythical frame painted by an illusion. The reality was even more alluring and mysterious than the farcical descriptions.

She turned to her left and ascended a side street which meandered up a hillside. Old cobblestones clicked beneath her heels as she made her way to the address on the tiny sheet of paper in her hand. She had not really looked with much thought at the address, but as the sun moved almost below the horizon she realized the ominous nature of the street name – Dark Hill Lane.

There seemed to be a darkness slowly creeping up the sloping steps, as if it was menacingly following her. She was used to darkness, the real darkness that resided in the hearts and minds of those minions of greed in a world where all the good things of life were reserved for the privileged class, where those at the very top of the economic ladder never had enough, always wanting more and had no compassion for those left behind by the evil of greed. Since an early age, she had dealt with that darkness that resided deep within far too many individuals. She understood that there were some people, far too many, who were dark to their cores, pitch black to the bone. This was the way of a cruel, inequitable, unjust world.

For Lynton, unique creature that she was, the difference between her darkness and other people's darkness was that she could look her own imperfections in the face and accept their existence and battle valiantly to overcome them, while most other people were covering their reflections in the recriminatory mirrors with white linen sheets to hide their inner selves. She always stood against injustice, while others accepted it, ignored it or participated in it. She realized that standing up for one's self was a declaration of freedom from those who wanted to despicably manipulate and exert wretched control. She refused to be restrained by convention or shame. She was a siren of sanity in a world of insane expectations. She was the wizard of wonder battling against those who stir the cauldron from hell, while wrapping themselves in the false sanctimonious hypocrisy of righteousness.

As she moved up the steep steps, her high heels were an impediment to smooth transitions from one step to the next, but her determined strides accentuated the tautness of her butt and her muscular calves. One could sense the utter softness of her silk-like dark skin that all men longed to touch and seductively stroke. She was breathtaking in her alluring beauty and her human spirit that seemed to emanate from her very core. Hers was the sort of beauty that you knew would not fade or grow jaded with time and years, but flourish, grow more radiant with life and its experience. Hers was a timeless beauty that would shine through wrinkles and age. She had an omnipresent air of confidence about her that accentuated secure, genuine sexiness that effervescently glowed as a result of the assuredness she exuded. Most women alone in a darkening and now nearly deserted place would exhibit fear, but in her demeanour one could sense a complete lack of alarm, which added to her magnetically tempestuous attractiveness.

Fate is a fickle partner. It is as if we are playing chess with fate our entire lives. Fate makes a move. We counter that move. For many of us playing the game, most times we have the feeling we cannot win, but still we continue with the game, for we cannot give up. Giving up is just not an option. Lynton felt that way as she reached the end of Dark Hill Lane. There were buildings in front of her, to the left and to the right. None had numbers on them. She was confused.

To her left were stairs leading up the side of a rug shop. For some reason, she felt drawn to those stairs as there seemed to be a glowing light filtering down from the top landing by a door. There appeared a sublime melancholia in that light escaping gently down the steps into the faint darkness. Was it possible that the flickering light was a festival of destiny dancing a celestial radiation to some infinite mystery that was luring Lynton to this place? Was there a sublime crucible waiting to be consummated by the fusion of two women, both lured by a mystical phone? Was this to be the merging of two souls into one space in pursuit of an unknown mystery? Should Lynton turn and run from what waited at the top of those stairs, run from fate? She perceived the fearful, but enchanting excitement that waited at the top of those stairs, as she imagined the forms of night, the winged strangers, the intrepid travelers of the invisible bending a throng of shadowy heads over the luminous building, luring her upward with the reflection of the human felicity on divine countenances. She could almost hear the rustling of confused, mysterious wings. Were they the wings of angels or the wings of demons?

<u>CHAPTER 3</u>
The Fingers of Fate

*Above the mist of a crescent moon
Something lays in wait to come down soon.
It feels like a disease without a cure,
A horrid nightmare to endure.*

*You can sense the evil it desires,
Stirring robustly hell's fires.
There is gripping fear about,
And in the throat is trapped a shout.*

*Like the feel of an icy tomb,
The soul senses impending doom!
Look up, down, left and right
For the evil one is coming into sight.*

Two Girls Who Danced
With the Demon of Darkness

The area where Lynton now stood looking upward had for hundreds of years been steeped in mystery and intrigue as historical reverence embraced the teeming mesh of humanity that had lived, toiled and died in the confines of this storied, bristling, cramped quarter of the city. Many, no most residents, had lived their entire lives in the confines of this place referred to as the Medina of Casablanca, an area maybe 20 hectares in size where all eyes gazed upon the streets, eyes belonging to people who were relegated to a meagre existence, but it was these people described by Karl Marx as the hopes of humanity who would hopefully one day rise in revolution to proclaim a workers' paradise. These noble beings were the natural proprietors of the streets; those who had not chosen their lowly existences, but had learned to adjust to their fates. In spite of their hardships, they had refused to bow down before their burdens, and made sacrifices for the betterment of all about them, extending a helping hand when those who lived in privilege would not. They experienced no petty selfishness, for their kindness was shared with all, their deeds living quietly as a testament to the sanctity of the human spirit as individuals worked year after year, decade after decade, century after century to lend the hand of compassion to their fellow sojourners on the path called life. Their deeds lived on quietly, unheralded as a perpetual monument over which was shed the hot tears of true nobility. Yet, there was evil incubating among them.

Two Girls Who Danced
With the Demon of Darkness

Lynton climbed the stairs stoically, still wondering why she was going in search of the woman who had bought that ancient phone, a relic that may have known words of joyous elation, phrases of misery, platitudes of praise, discordant evil machinations of sinister plotters, even plans for murder. She had once bought a new cell-phone, about which her husband wrote a best-selling book, a phone that had plagued her night and day with the voice from beyond the grave, a voice that informed her of impending doom. Was she fearful that this was a father, a mother, a brother or a sister of that cell-phone, which also portended impending evil?

Reluctant to knock, she stood just staring at the door. Its ancient holm, cork and oak combination weaved intricately into an almost tapestry of the past glaring back at her. She contemplated turning and walking away. Long ago, she had promised her husband to avoid getting involved with mysteries, with searching for demons, with causing him worry over her propensity for putting herself in danger. Yet, this was just a situation of idle curiosity. Surely there was no danger here. Yes, she was going to meet Jasmine Alexander, of whom her husband had written about based on second hand information from his detective friend, Aaron Adams, but it was just curiosity from realizing that there was a phone from an antique store she had once visited in West Hollywood, a store where she had encountered a portly Belgium of a somewhat dubious nature.

Two Girls Who Danced
With the Demon of Darkness

If only it had all been that simple! If only evil people somewhere insidiously committing evil deeds could be separated from normal society and corralled in a pen of repentant remorse where their deeds of malevolence would be purified, but the line dividing good and evil cut through the heart of every human being, and who would be willing to destroy a piece of his or her own heart? The line separating good and evil passes through every human heart. This line shifts; it oscillates with each passing day. And even within hearts overwhelmed by evil, one small bridgehead of good is retained deep within; but to purge any evil was a monumental task, even in the best of all hearts, because there was a small corner where evil could be bred. Lynton was as pure an individual as had every breathed, but even she recognized her own faults. Yet, one fault she never entertained – accepting malevolence in any form. She had built a reputation for standing against vileness, wickedness and villainy ever since she was a little girl. She took a deep breath and with much trepidation knocked gently on the door, almost hoping there would be no response. Hearing the patter of footsteps from within, her heart raced with the anticipation of meeting Jasmine Alexander.

The door slowly opened and there Jasmine Alexander stood. Who else could it be? She was older than Lynton had expected. Why shouldn't she be? It had been thirteen years since the infamous whirlwind incident. Anyway, years bring the wisdom of time, the strength of experience. With each year flowed acquired knowledge as a guide to accepting deeper meaning to things that might have once had no meaning. Jasmine, no doubt, had gained depth to her character by the good and bad arms she had fallen into, the shoulders she leaned on for solace and the hearts that were opened with warmth. Thus was the ageing process for learned, extraordinary women. That was experience that stays in the soul and shines in the eyes. Yet, one could see sadness in those eyes. The sadness that said she had loved and lost, but accepted it as a price worth paying.

Jasmine was still a beautiful woman, but the toll of living on the run, living on the edge for so long had plagued her soul, plagued her in a way that had added wrinkles to her brow and an obvious strain on her heart. Standing there, the much taller Jasmine looked down at Lynton and let out a long sigh before she offered, "Lynton Viñas, I have seen your picture in Wayne Frye's books. What on earth are you doing here?"

Surprised that she would be recognized by Jasmine, Lynton stood dumbfounded for maybe two or three seconds before saying, "I am here to speak to you about a phone you bought from Abi Mohammad."

Stepping to one side, Jasmine, with a glowing smile said, "Come in."

She pointed to a sofa, indicating Lynton should take a seat. As Lynton did so, Jasmine eased into a rocker. The two women stared at one another in silence before Lynton finally said, "You do still have the phone?"

"I have it yes," she replied as she pointed to a small table beside her bed, where the phone sat. "I was fascinated by it, but I have been reluctant to pick up the receiver. I have read Frye's book *Lynton Buys a New Cell Phone and Hears the Voice of Doom.* Maybe that is why I am reluctant to pick up the receiver, because I know what happened to you in Manila when you got a new cell phone."

"That is true. It was one of the most harrowing experiences of my life, but there was another incident that happened later and has not been written about. There was another phone, an antique phone like yours. Maybe it was yours. I saw it in an antique shop years ago in Manhattan down in Greenwich Village. I held the receiver to my ear, and I heard a voice whisper to me, whisper something that has always bothered me, always made me curious about antique phones."

"And what was said?"

"Faites attention ma chérie, car il y a encore des démons dans le monde."

Jasmine leaned slightly forward and with a trembling voice said, "In English, be careful my dear, for there are still demons in the world."

"Yes, so you speak French."

"This is Morocco. Of course I speak some French. I lived in Meknes for awhile, which was the headquarters of the French Foreign Legion in this nation."

Two Girls Who Danced
With the Demon of Darkness

Lynton knew that every person is part of a system that flows and communicates between their brain and their body, between their brain and other brains, between their brain and the environment. She understood that the brains we are born with continue to mature and change. Change is always possible, because we are constantly evolving. So, to see a person, to really see them you need a wide vision of instinct that is linked up with senses of empathy, creativity and logic.

She immediately assessed Jasmine Alexander as an astute individual with a logically oriented mind and great empathy for those burdened by the unfair economic system that relegated the majority of humanity to always be on the outside looking in. Jasmine was also a person who loved deeply and honestly, which is why she had left Aaron Adams. Left him in order to protect him.

Looking at the phone, Lynton said, "Do you believe in demons?"

Smiling, Jasmine replied, "Maybe I should be asking you that. After all, you are a famous demon hunter."

"Famous? Well, maybe, but I am not even sure I believe in demons, although I have come up against forces that have left me thoroughly dumbfounded when trying to find an explanation, left me questioning my own sanity sometimes. What I have learned in my life is that the worst demons are not flying around with horns sticking out of their heads; they are walking around in suits, sitting behind desks in skyscrapers affecting people's lives with the evil of their greed. They are in pulpits on Sunday mornings promoting finger-pointing hatred rather than love. They are people of influence and power who neglect the needs of the less fortunate, the forgotten, the put-upon who are on their knees begging for some fairness. The real demons are walking among us every single day, and they are winning the battle against good and evil."

"You are very eloquent, as eloquent as you are described in the books about you."

"It is easy to be eloquent when you are passionate about things."

Taking a very deep breath, Jasmine said, "But you are here because of a phone. Why does it interest you so much? Surely it cannot be just because you heard something whispered to you over a phone in an antique store in Greenwich Village long ago. Maybe it wasn't anything but your imagination."

"I have a vivid imagination, but the truth is I know it wasn't my imagination, and I have an important question to ask you."

"Ask."

"In that shop here or outside it, did you encounter a portly European?"

A puzzled look slowly grew upon her face, as Jasmine replied timidly, "Yes, but he did not speak. Before I bought the phone, I saw a portly European man pointing at it. I blinked my eyes and he was gone, seemingly disappearing into thin air."

Two Girls Who Danced
With the Demon of Darkness

It was then that Lynton felt the need to unburden herself from something that had plagued her for years. "Well, the truth is when I went into that shop in Greenwich Village so many years ago, as I was entering I bumped into a portly gentleman, who said nothing, but just smiled at me. The same gentleman was browsing around the Hollywood curio shop I entered a few years later. I noticed him immediately, but I looked down at an old clock, and when I looked up he was gone. Then, right here in Casablanca, as I was entering Abi Mohammad's shop he was coming out. He said nothing, but gave me a wink. I walked through the doorway sideways because of his girth. Then, when I got inside I turned to see where he was headed. He was gone. Seemed to just disappear, as you indicated, into thin air."

Jasmine, offered with a quivering quizzical voice, "He was a very portly man of about fifty I'd say. For some reason, he seemed familiar. Not that I knew him personally, but that he was someone whom I knew without ever having met him, maybe someone I heard about or read about. And his clothes, he was dressed in a suit that looked like it was from the 1930's."

A light seemed to go on in Lynton's mind. It brought some clarity to what had been a mystery, but its clarity would itself be a mystery. Looking puzzled, she said to Jasmine, "Have you ever read any of Agatha Christie's books?"

The same light seemed to go on in Jasmine's head. "Of course, I have read that man's description many times in her books. Incredible isn't it? But it can't be. No way can it be. He is a fictional character, and even if he wasn't he would be dead by now."

"Dead or not, Hercule Poirot," offered a shocked Lynton.

A befuddled Jasmine said, "The portly Belgium detective in Agatha Christie's novels. But, like I said, he'd be dead if he was real."

Lynton, now staring over at the phone, seemed to drift into a sort of trance. "We have to pick up the earpiece on that phone."

Jasmine got up and moved tepidly toward the phone with Lynton behind her. They both took a seat on the edge of the bed, and Jasmine held the phone base in her left hand and lifted the receiver with her right hand, tilting it slightly so she could share the earpiece with Lynton the two of them just waited and waited and waited. It seemed like it was minutes they sat there with their ears near the receiver, but it was only seconds. Suddenly, an extremely accented voice said, "Ah, you finally have found the courage to pick up the receiver. I, Hercule Poirot, have been waiting patiently to find the right individual to delve into a mystery for the ages. Ironically, I now have two of the most determined seekers of truth upon planet earth. I shall detail for you a mystery that has led my spirit and this phone to the very den of inequity here in the Old City of Casablanca. You shall be mystified, scared and intrigued by what you are about to encounter."

Two Girls Who Danced
With the Demon of Darkness

He cleared his throat and continued, "In Casablanca, which I visited long ago, subsequently journeying across the desert from Cairo after my harrowing adventure described in *Death on the Nile* in the 1937 novel by Agatha Christie, there is a mystery that needs to be solved, and there appears no one more qualified than you two to undertake solving it. I am fortunate two such astute investigative minds as yours have seemingly merged. Your investigative skills are almost equal to those of the great Hercule Poirot."

There was boastfulness in his voice, and why not? After all, as of the publication of this present story, over two billion copies of Agatha Christie's Hercule Poirot mysteries have been sold.

The voice was silent for a few seconds before continuing, "Dr. Martin Herloin right here in the Old City is the key to a profound mystery that needs solving. I will tell you more of him later. Other great detectives will communicate with you, and help solve this mystery. Pick this phone up regularly so that I may lend you assistance and know the fate of the investigation."

The phone went dead, and the two women stared at one another in complete and utter disbelief as Jasmine very gently placed the phone down on the table. The word *weird* could not adequately describe how the two women felt, as they just sat in silence.

When Lynton left, she parted with an understanding that she would return the next day. Walking down the steps in confusion over what had occurred, as she reached the last step she realized it was awful to be caught up in a game and have no idea what the game and its rules were. That very moment Lynton realized that in so many of her adventures at times of great calamity and utter confusion clarity of purpose was slow in coming. This time was no different, because she had learned over time that the supernatural is often the natural not understood, and that phone did indeed involve the supernatural.

Still, she knew that the purest ore was produced by the hottest fire and that the roaring thunder-bolt was created by the darkest storm, and that somehow this was going to be an adventure that would produce a blazing fire and clamouring thunder that would rock the very foundations of Old City Casablanca, because she looked at her life as a grand adventure written by the fingers of fate.

**Two Girls Who Danced
With the Demon of Darkness**

<u>CHAPTER 4</u>
Uneasiness Griped Them

*A demon loves secret visits
With meetings quite dolorous.
His smile and glance mysterious.*

*He rails with caustic sermons,
Pouring forth frozen poison in the soul.
With endless slandering tirades,
He loves when the sun fades.*

*He claims that beauty is but a dream.
He has no faith in love or freedom.
He looks on life with ridicule,
And in the whole of this life
He only wants to spread strife.*

Two Girls Who Danced
With the Demon of Darkness

The next day, the two girls picked up the phone together again, sharing the earpiece. A heavily accented voice that they assumed was genuinely Hercule Poirot, though he was only fictional in nature, said, "111 Gloom Way here in the Old City." The phone then went dead and the two women stared at one another in questioning dismay.

Lynton said, "Let's go."

Not verbally replying, Jasmine nodded her head affirmatively and the two women set out for 111 Gloom Way, which Jasmine knew was nearby, and which they would eventually learn was appropriately named.

The trek there took them through an area filled with jocularity as the street people were enjoying some sort of festival, which was common for the Old City. Still, there was a tension one could feel present, as they entered a square just on the outskirts of Gloom Way, where people were dancing, most of them wearing masks of various varieties. Lynton had always been leery of masks on people, believing that wearing masks was never a good sign. Maybe it was the anonymity and the obvious uncanny nature of not knowing what kind of person was behind the mask, or perhaps it was the decades of horror movies ingraining a deep sense of distrust about someone wearing a mask outside of a masquerade ball. Yet, Lynton knew that even without a mask people were often hiding behind a facade, making their natural faces masks of sorts. The world was full of monsters hiding behind friendly faces. Like icebergs, people tended to only expose a small part of themselves, and it was what lay beneath the surface, beneath the mask that was deadliest. It was true that virtue only wore a veil but vice a mask.

Exactly how does an evil entity manifest itself? Does it just pop out of nowhere or materialize bit by bit? How does it move? Does it drift about or actually walk and create the sound of footsteps? Is it gauzy and see through or more solid in appearance? Does it give off some type of eerie glow? How is it dressed? Is it in old fashioned clothes or something that is more modern? What about facial features and the hair? What sounds does it make? Can one hear it breathing? Wait, does it actually breathe?

Those were the thoughts going through Lynton's mind as a man wrapped in a flowing dark cape and wearing a grotesque devil's mask approached them. The mask was so realistic it actually seemed to be his face. His lips hardly moved, as looking at Jasmine he said, "Shall we dance my lovely?"

He did not give her a chance to say yes or no. He grabbed her arms, and they began to glide about the square. After about a minute, they danced over to Lynton. The man let go of Jasmine and bowed to Lynton, "And now it is your turn my lovely."

Not giving Lynton a chance to reply either, he took her in his strong arms and glided about the square with her. Not as timid as Jasmine, Lynton said, as they were dancing, "Do I not know you, sir?"

In a scratchy, soft, almost whispering voice, he replied, "Everybody knows me."

As they danced back to where Jasmine was standing watching them, he bowed almost majestically and gently but determinedly said to them, "You ladies should be very careful with your intrepid curiosity. Remember that curiosity killed the cat, and the same can apply to curious humans."

He stopped, turned and walked slowly into a raucous passing crowd. Jasmine and Lynton quizzically gazed at one another. They were totally dumbfounded by the unusual encounter with a man who seemed sinister at best.

"Strange man," offered Jasmine.

"Very," replied Lynton.

They turned to look for the man who had casually walked away, but he was gone. He had completely disappeared from view. They could not see him anywhere in the square.

For most people, life is not the truth they want, but an illusion they learn to live with. That is why so many people spend their lives chasing the fantasy that success is a fine home, a new luxury car, designer clothes and all the other trappings that say, "I made it, and I am important." Lynton and Jasmine were not of that ilk; they concluded that civilization as it exists today is like a thin layer of ice upon a deep ocean of chaos and darkness. They both realized they had just danced with somebody or some thing that was an agent of that chaos and darkness.

Two Girls Who Danced
With the Demon of Darkness

Lynton said, "We are running late. We need to find 111 Gloom Way. Wish my GPS would work here."

Smiling, Jasmine offered an opinion she had formed after several years living in Old City. "Here, you learn to live the old way. I generally prefer that to the modern world."

Sighing, Lynton replied, "In modern society, where most people live in cities, and where both needs and wishes are absolved through the same remote agency, which is money, the distinction between wishes and needs has altogether vanished. And yes, I feel here a sense that people are not as lost as they are in the outside world, especially in the west, where greed is the motivation that oils the machinery of capitalism, which grinds the average person up and spits them out into misery."

"You sound like my dear former lover, Aaron Adams."

Taking a deep breath, Lynton said, "A wise man is he, which is why my husband writes about him so often."

As they started walking away from the square, Jasmine, in a very forlorn voice said, "Ah, it seems so long ago, like centuries, when I wrapped myself in Aaron's arms and felt the glory of his love and wisdom."

Lynton reached out and took Jasmine's hand and philosophized. "In the arithmetic of love, one plus one equals everything, and two minus one equals nothing. I, too, have loved and lost, so I understand your pain. There is no love like a lost love and no pain like a broken heart. Still, I found my love after failing three times. Do not give up, because when you least expect it, love will somehow find you again."

Smiling, Jasmine said, "You are indeed a wise woman, Lynton."

"Wise enough to know," she said as she pointed to a street sign nearby, "where Gloom Way is."

There before them was a winding street going upward. It was covered in darkness, but not the darkness of night. It was bleaker than night. A feeling hung over the entrance to the street like a dark curtain that had descended to protect the place from intruders. Where they stood looking at the street, the air was clear and crisp. But on Gloom Way there was a thick layer of fog. So thick that it appeared it would encumber the ability to breathe. Fog was everywhere on that dark street, fog that seemed to hold everything in its tight embrace. It flowed into the few doorways they could see. It crept up outside walls and seemed to move slowly and distinctly among a solitary figure, a man wearing a black cloak like the one that had been worn by the person they had danced with in the square. The man was shrouded in that cloak with a turned up collar hiding the back of his neck. He stopped, turned to look back down the street at the two women. The mask was gone, but he appeared more sinister without it. His red, burning eyes seemed set upon swollen flesh as he stared at them.

Two Girls Who Danced
With the Demon of Darkness

He turned back and started walking up the street, a small overhead light casting an eerie glow down on him. He turned the corner and disappeared.

Lynton had often contemplated that perhaps the explanation for all the pain in the world was the fact that maybe earth was actually another planet's hell, with people sent here unaware that they were sojourning in hell. At the very moment she and Jasmine were slowly moving up the dark street toward number 111, she felt an absolutely indescribable sense of menace. It was hell, really hell on earth to be there at that very moment, but there was no turning back. The both of them, as they held hands to gain courage, sensed that there was something waiting at 111 Gloom Way that was monstrously ugly, filthy, dark and sinister.

As they passed under the overhead light, the street curved to the right and there leaning against the side of a building was a suave looking black man with a look of fearlessness on his face. He appeared a man who took no shit from anybody. Instinctively, Lynton and Jasmine knew he could handle a gun and his fists. Also, he was a ladies' man they sensed by the way his lips curled as he said, "And what are two fine ladies doing out by yourselves on Gloom Way?"

Lynton recognized the man. She knew who he was. She gave Jasmine a knowing look as she said to him, "We're looking for 111."

"Could be a dangerous place for someone unprepared."

Lynton, remembering dialogue from the movie, *Shaft*, couldn't resist herself and said, "Who's the black private dick that's a sex machine to all the chicks?"

He replied, "Shaft."

She said, "You damn right. And whose the man who'll risk his life for a brother?"

"Shaft." He said. "Can you dig it?"

"They say this cat Shaft is a real, real bad mother…."

"Shut your mouth," come back a smiling reply. "You talkin' about Shaft."

Two Girls Who Danced
With the Demon of Darkness

"Yep, talking about John Shaft. What you doing here?"

"I'm here because I'm always where there's a mystery, where's there's trouble, where there's strife, where there's evil to be confronted. I'm here to tell you that your universe and its contents are not just dreams, visions, fiction! Strange, because they are so frankly and hysterically insane like a God who could have made good children as easily as bad, yet preferred to make bad ones; who insisted they prize their bitter lives, yet stingily cut them short; who gave his angels eternal happiness unearned, yet required his other children to earn it; who gave his angels painless lives, yet cursed his other children with biting miseries and maladies of mind and body; who mouthed justice and invented hell, mouthed mercy and invented the devil, mouthed golden rules, and forgiveness multiplied by seventy times seven, but sends sinners to purgatory; who mouthed morals to other people and had none himself; who frowned upon crimes, yet committed them all; who created man without invitation, then tried to shuffle the responsibility for man's acts upon man, instead of honourably placing it where it belonged, upon himself; and finally, with altogether divine obtuseness, invented the poor, the abused slaves he made to worship him. There is no heaven, but there very definitely is a hell and you are about to enter it if you are brave enough."

Jasmine, confused, was silent in bewilderment. Lynton turning her back, ignoring the man standing there for a second, said to Jasmine, "This man is John Shaft. Surely you know him?"

"You mean the movie private eye. John Shaft? He is a fictional character, not real."

"You just saw him didn't you? That's real enough for me."

"Yes."

They both turned their heads and the man was gone, disappeared. They looked at one another again quizzically, trying to understand what had just happened. They couldn't.

Lynton, shrugging her shoulders, and seeing a house number to their left that read 33, pointed upward. They walked up the dark, fog-laden, foreboding, cobblestone street in confusion.

Two Girls Who Danced
With the Demon of Darkness

When a traveler in confusion comes upon a lonely and curious place maybe the correct action would be to retrace their steps and leave. That kind of reaction was not in either woman's DNA. They were made of sterner stuff.

The ground got higher, and the brier-bordered stone walls pressed closer and closer against the ruts of the dusty, curving, cobblestone road. The place was mostly devoid of people and seemed particularly barren; while the houses and places of business wore a surprisingly uniform aspect of age, squalor and dilapidation. Without knowing why, one hesitated to ask directions from the very few gnarled, solitary figures spying at them from crumbling doorways. The figures were so silent and furtive that one felt they somehow harboured knowledge of forbidden things, with which it would be better to have nothing to do. A feeling of strange uneasiness pervaded among the two curious women. There was a complete lack of comfort and naturalness, and sometimes the sky silhouetted dancing dark shadows in queer circles among the stone buildings.

There was a problematical depth of fear in the way they walked, and one sensed a feeling of dubious safety. When the road dipped and they nearly stumbled, fear crept upon them like a sly parasite of consternation. Dark clouds above them seemed stationary and the fog crept up to their thighs, as if enveloping them in a misty vice.

It appeared that most of the houses among the few business establishments were deserted and falling to ruin, and a broken-down small mosque harboured a slovenly mercantile establishment that was closed, but one could see a lone merchant inside tidying up. A dark shadowy skywalk connecting two buildings was now over them as they continued there ascent upward. After they passed under the skywalk, it was hard to prevent the impression of a faint, malignant-type odour about the street. It was the odour of mould, decay and death.

Outsiders visited this section of Old City Casablanca as seldom as possible and one could almost believe that there should be signs posted regarding the dark nature of the place they were now traversing. The scenery, judged by any ordinary aesthetic canon, was more than commonly foreboding. It certainly made one feel that this little world, along with the world outside, was a place filled with evil, where the strong preyed on the weak and thus the rich preyed on the poor. It solidified the idea that there was no God, because how could a God exist that allowed the evil which was so unchecked and so prevalent? Oh, but this place certainly made you feel there was a hell, because you just knew you were about to enter it!

Centuries ago, when talk of witches, Satan-worshipers and strange ghostly presences were not laughed at it was the custom to give reasons for avoiding the locality in which the two women found themselves. In the assumedly more sensible current age, there was little talk of such things.

Two Girls Who Danced
With the Demon of Darkness

People were supposedly too sophisticated in the modern world for such nonsense. Yet, there was a dark undercurrent in today's Old City that seemed to be simmering beneath the surface.

The closest anything came to such suspiciously nonsensical horror was in 1918 when something called the Casablanca Horror occurred. It was hushed up as much as possible. Perhaps one reason was that the natives of Old City Casablanca were, at the present time, having gone far along that path of retrogression in Casablanca's most backward area, reticent to drag up the past evil that had occurred there long ago, an evil that was supposedly conjured up from hell itself when a minion of Satan was rumoured to be roaming about Old City causing mayhem. It was a time when an evil entity was supposedly forming a coven with the well-defined mental and physical stigma of degeneracy and inbreeding that a few of the residents were actively engaging in as a part of devil worship. There were rumours of overt viciousness and of half-hidden murders, incestuous relationships and deeds of almost unnameable violence and perversity. The old style gentry kept somewhat above the general level of decay; though many branches sunk into the sordid populace practicing all kinds of debauchery.

No one, even those who had the facts concerning the recent horrors that were slowly cropping up again, could say just what the problem was in Old City, though old legends spoke of unhallowed rites and conclaves of devil worshippers amidst the small populace of devotees hiding in the shadows of the area. There were a few Imams who spoke out against the coming terror that was expected if people did not reform. Of course, they always had railed against Beelzebub and Belial as demons in search of souls to capture.

The two determined ladies stood in awe as the site of a building loomed in front of them. They suddenly sensed a very plain discourse of evil at 111 Gloom Way now to their right. Then they heard a gravely voice with a Chinese accent behind them. "Remember ladies that one small wind can raise much dust."

They turned and there was famed oriental detective, Charlie Chan. In shock at his presence, they stood in awe as he said, "Curiosity is why a cat has nine lives, because curiosity can be a killer. Are you sure you want to knock on the door of that house?" All the time he was pointing at the nefarious looking building 111 Gloom Way that stood eerily in the darkness.

Lynton, having watched many of what she called 19-forgotten movies with her husband blurted out, "You're Charlie Chan."

"It is a wise woman who can remember faces from old movies. Old movies offer entertainment not found in movies today."

"That is certainly right my honourable friend. Are you here to help us or to warn us?"

"A bit of both I suppose. Remember Confucius said that man who seeks trouble never finds it far off. Same applies to ladies."

Two Girls Who Danced
With the Demon of Darkness

Jasmine chimed in, "We have no idea why we are even here. We are just following the directions of a detective called Hercule Poiret."

"A wise man is he. Just be aware that much evil can enter a small space. Be cognizant that patience is big sister to wisdom, and you will both need patience in solving a dilemma that has been around for years."

He then pointed to the house and they turned to look back at it. In near whisper he said behind their backs, "Confucius say that a house is not always a home."

They turned back and he, like John Shaft, had disappeared.

Charlie Chan Image ©Twentieth Century Fox

Two Girls Who Danced
With the Demon of Darkness

Again bewildered, the two took a deep breath and moved gingerly toward the house, which was becoming clearer now as the fog had lifted.

*The clearing fog did not diminish
the sinister looking nature of the house.*

Moving onto the sidewalk as they neared the house, Jasmine astutely observed an incredibly distinguished looking gentleman and an obviously sophisticated lady across the street. They were in clothes which appeared to be from the 1930's or 1940's. The gentleman was immaculately attired in a tuxedo and the lady was exquisitely dressed. The man was motioning for them to come across the street.

Two Girls Who Danced
With the Demon of Darkness

Lynton, sensing she had seen them before, said to Jasmine as she began crossing the street, "Come on. Let's see what they want. This is turning out to be one weird night."

The man, a distinguished looking dandy, attired in a tuxedo, had a look of sophistication about him along with a sense of mystery. The lady by his side was magnificently slender, with dark short hair that glistened from the shimmering light bouncing off it as a result of the nearby lamppost's glare. Class was written all over her, and you knew immediately, despite an intelligent looking husband, she was the real brains of the pair with a snappy sense of timing and a haughty attitude that was not obnoxious but still intimidating.

Lynton said to them as they approached the two, "What can we do for you?"

The lady replied, "I am Nora Charles and this is my husband Nick. Perhaps we can do something for you."

Somewhat shocked with the realization that she was face-to-face with two of the most famous movie detectives, Lynton, having been forced to watch them in movies from the golden age of Hollywood by her husband, looked at Jasmine and said, "Meet the greatest husband and wife detectives in cinema history."

It was at that point when Nick said in his precise English, "Not just great my dear, but also the best."

Lynton replied, "I stand in awe, sir."

"Well, you should," replied Nick.

Two Girls Who Danced
With the Demon of Darkness

"Don't mind my husband," interjected Nora. "He is feeling gnarly, because I've made him stay sober tonight."

With a whimsical sarcastic tone, Nick said, "My wife can put two and two together sometimes and get four, but fails to realize other times it can be twenty-two. You ladies are about to encounter a mystery that gets 22 from 2 plus 2. Are you sure you want to knock on the door to that house?"

Lynton replied, "We aren't sure after all the warnings we have been getting from some very well-respected people, although I am not so sure they are not just figments of our vivid imaginations."

Nora said, "The exercise of imagination is dangerous to those who profit from the way things are, because it has the power to show that the way things are is not always permanent. There are forces at work here that have, unfortunately, been permanent in this world far too long. Evil is a fixture that has a firm grip on the world – the evil of greed which defeats the good that should abound. The evil of ignorance. Not ignorance in the sense of lack of schooling. Nor ignorance in the sense of lack of intelligence, but the conscious and unconscious decisions by people to take for granted what they read or watch as fact without bothering to fact-check and confirm sources, to take opinion and redefine it as fact, to confuse statistical probability for factual certainty, and to assume those with belief systems other than their own are by definition wrong, dangerous and/or need to be changed or educated to accept one's own belief systems as facts. You ladies are about to face the unbelievable, so we just want you to be prepared for evil of the most insidious kind."

Nick interjected, "The world is a dangerous place, not just because of the people who do evil, but because of people who see evil and do nothing about it. My guess is that our friend Hercule Poirot selected you two for this dangerous assignment, because you see evil and are willing to confront it. We just want you forewarned that the horror you are about to face will try your souls."

"We don't even know what we are going to face," replied Jasmine. "We only have an address, nothing else. We are blind to the reason we are even here, except our curiosity about an old phone that somehow wound up with me, and then we hear somebody claiming to be Hercule Poirot on that phone telling us to go to Gloom Way. I wish I had never bought the damn thing."

Nora, a note of extreme seriousness in her tone said, "There is so much about fate that you cannot control, but other things do fall under your jurisdiction. You can decide how to spend your time, whom you interact with, whom you share your body with and what you spend your money and energy on. You can select what you read and eat and study. You can choose how you're going to regard unfortunate circumstances in your life, and whether you will see those circumstances as curses or opportunities. You can choose your words and the tone of voice in which you speak to

Two Girls Who Danced
With the Demon of Darkness

others. And most of all, you can choose your thoughts. However, it is the fate of most people who mingle with the world to sometimes, on rare occasions, actually come across that which is unfathomable and unexplainable. You are about to face that situation, but you are two women of character who have known adversity and survived. Just know that fate put you here because of an antique telephone. You were picked to confront an unimaginable evil. Be extremely vigilant and remember that your courage will see you through."

Nick and Nora then joined hands, turned and started walking back down the street from whence Lynton and Jasmine came. Jasmine and Lynton stared at one another in bewilderment. When they looked back down the street, Nick and Nora had disappeared. Uneasiness gripped them.

Nick and Nora Charles
(Myrna Loy and William Powell ©MGM)

CHAPTER 5
Challenge of Monumental Proportions

*There are demons and evil spirits
Lurking in the shadows of our minds and hearts.
Some small forgotten corner is where it starts.
It only takes a single little crack
For the evil to take root and attack.
It eats away slowly, carefully biding its time,
Until it is too late as you think you are fine.
It starts small: softening the edges
Bit by bit, shifting, driving wedges.
It is a poison sweeping through;
A silent deadly killer it is true,
But worst of all it affects the greater whole.
It takes a soul as pure and white as snow,
And works to turn it black as coal.*

Two Girls Who Danced
With the Demon of Darkness

Trepidation set in as the two women stared across the street at the house where evil obviously dwelt. Certain houses, like certain persons, manage somehow to proclaim at once their character for evil. It was obvious that there was something radically amiss with the place; something sinister waited whoever might enter. There was an atmosphere of wickedness that menacingly permeated from that house. There was vileness about it, almost as if it was diseased and the disease was contagious to all who might dare enter.

As they approached the steps to the house, there came into their nostrils foul odours, and the rushing but subdued air of a howling noise that seemed to be warning them to flee. However, it was too late. Lynton grabbed the knocker, and as if she was afraid of being too noisy she very gently pounded the knocker almost hoping no one would answer.

The door was slowly opened and what was assumed to be a man servant stood before them. Lynton said, "We have no idea why we are here, but could we see the master of the house?"

"Mr. Beale is in conference, but do come in and take a seat," he said as he pointed to two large double doors on the right, walked to them and swung them open.

A long narrow room, opening into a huge library, stretched before them. The room was decorated in magnificence, although it was a bit bright with the colour red predominating. There were shiny parquet floors, crystal mirrors all about and lavish antique furniture accentuated by solid gold braided draperies.

The exquisite grandeur of the room faded in their minds as a glorious vision of mysterious beauty sashayed in like a queen approaching her throne. The young woman had poise, charm and adroitness that was instantly apparent without her speaking a word. She was glamorous, slender, curvy, mature, willowy, fashionable and exhibited a haughtiness that made one think she considered herself superior in every way. Meanwhile, right behind her was a tall man with a determined stride. He looked totally unsurprised by the presence of Lynton and Jasmine.

Lynton said, "We apologize for bursting in on you, but we have a strange tale to tell about why we are here. The truth is that we don't really know why we are here."

"Well, maybe you are just destined to be here," he said as he turned to his lady friend. "This is Marian Laveau and I am Nicholas Beale, but please call me Nick."

"I am Lynton Viñas and this is my friend Jasmine Alexander."

"Pleased Ms. Alexander," he said while bowing his head to her, "and you my dear Ms. Viñas are well known. I have seen your pictures in magazines, newspapers and television. I have read your husband's books, most of them at least."

"I am flattered you have heard of me," replied Lynton.

Two Girls Who Danced
With the Demon of Darkness

"I think you are used to recognition, my dear. It goes with the territory – a territory you enjoy exploring," said Mr. Beale. "Being a famed demon hunter is more a calling than a profession."

"Ah, you know my penchant for exploring mysteries, then."

A gleam in his eye, Beale replied, "I do, and I hope you are not here to investigate me and this house, as there is nothing very mysterious going on here."

"Well, truthfully, and I am sure you will find it hard to believe, it was an old telephone from the 1930's that got me here, and someone, I assume perhaps impersonating a famous private detective named Hercule Poirot."

"I know of Poirot. Quiet famous is he, but also very dead if he actually existed."

"Yes," replied Lynton, "if he was real, he would indeed be dead."

At that point, Ms. Laveau, in an abrupt manner, said in a sarcastic tone, "We have guests Nick, and I think we have neglected them long enough. Perhaps you should show these ladies out."

Beale's greyish eyes pierced daggers Laveau's way, but she gave him a derisive stare that seemed to make him wilt. He motioned toward the door, "I'll show you ladies out. You can come again when I am not entertaining guests."

Noticing several crates in the adjoining dining room, Jasmine, as they headed toward the front door said, "Looks like someone is moving in or moving out."

Two Girls Who Danced
With the Demon of Darkness

Marian Laveau very derisively said, "That doesn't concern you." She then looked directly at Nick and said, "We must join our guests."

Nick said with a wink, "Drop by another time ladies. Oh, by the way, I enjoyed our dance."

Across the hallway was a large dinning room with people seated around the table. Lynton, observed two men standing by a fireplace, one tall and extremely thin with coarse brown hair and the other an albino with piercing pink eyes. At the table was a man with flowing, long white hair who seemed to be audibly muttering to himself. Also seated at the table was an Asian with cold, penetrating eyes that were wilfully staring at the two ladies, a very dark man obviously of Berber origin and finally a thin woman with spindly legs and an upturned snarl on her moist lips.

As Lynton and Jasmine were slowly walking out, the door was slammed behind them with a thud that seemed to shake the house. Although Nick had been somewhat cordial, it was obvious that Marian Laveau was not pleased with their appearance that had apparently interrupted some type of meeting. There suddenly came a whining from inside far behind the door. The whining indicated someone was in deep pain as it rose loftily through the thick door. Its impact was more pronounced, as in the distance down the street came a sound of rolling thunder accompanied by hoarse murmurs of some type of cadence from a recitation inside the house that seemed to mingle with a hollow breeze that was sweeping up the steps where the two ladies stood bewildered and confused.

While going down the steps of the stoop, they heard a tapping at a window from the second floor. It was a stranger, and he raised the window and tossed out a note that fell at Lynton's feet. She picked it up and it simply read: "Don't come back. It is dangerous."

As the two of them retraced their steps back down the street, they did so in befuddled silence, until Lynton said with great concern, "There is some very queer business going on in that house. I am not sure you should pursue this any further, but my curiosity is piqued. I will understand if you don't want to continue with this."

"Don't be ridiculous," was Jasmine's reply.

Smiling, Lynton said with determination, "Done!"

For Lynton, she lived by the simple observation she once heard a teacher in graduate school relate: "It is far better to grasp the universe as it really is than to persist in delusion, however satisfying and reassuring that delusion might be." Yet, she realized that delusions were what kept people enslaved. Was Nick Beale enslaved by a delusion or was he actually the delusion?

It was the same teacher who had, in private, told her about Donald Trump's ability to convince people to support a buffoon when he related that one of the saddest lessons of history was that if people have been bamboozled long enough they tend to reject any evidence of the bamboozle.

Two Girls Who Danced
With the Demon of Darkness

They are no longer interested in finding out the truth. The bamboozle completely captures them. It was simply too painful to acknowledge they had been taken. Thus, once a charlatan is given power over you, you almost never get it back. Was that woman, Marian Laveau, exercising some mystical power over Nick Beale or were they co-conspirators?

The two ladies parted company, but the next day Lynton had breakfast with Jasmine, and the two discussed the strange happenings they had observed. They were determined to return and somehow speak more candidly with Nick Beale. As they were having breakfast, a man, bearing a striking resemblance to Humphrey Bogart, came over to their table and asked if he might take a seat.

They cordially, with surprised looks over the familiarity of the man's appearance, motioned for him to take a seat. He did, easing into the chair with the assurance of a Greek God who had just descended from Mount Olympus. Lynton, having had to endure watching old movies from the 1930's and 1940's with her husband, who was much older the she was, immediately connected the rugged good looks of the man to a character from the movie The Maltese Falcon, a movie she had seen many times.

He said to the two women, "I am a private eye. Spade is the name – Sam Spade."

Looks of astonishment passed between Lynton and Jasmine. Was the guy joking? After all, if there really was a Sam Spade, he would be over 100. The guy must be putting them on, but he was doing a good job of it, as his clothes looked like they had been pulled from wardrobe in central casting as he, despite the heat of Casablanca, wore a light coloured trench coat which contrasted with the dark pants, white dress shirt, and solid dark tie. His unmistakable grey hat with a black band was worn angled and low over one eye. He removed it and placed it on the table in front of him as the waiter came over, and asked if he could get him something.

He replied, "Too early for bourbon, so I guess a strong black coffee will give me the boost I need."

The waiter bowed slightly and left as he was saying, "Yes sir."

Lynton had enough experience with the police and various nefarious characters in her many adventures to realize from the slight bulge in his coat that underneath it was a gun shoulder holster, probably made of tan leather to carry his deadly .38 special. Oh, and the final assurance that this guy was the real deal from the 1940's were his plain black, lace-up shoes that were immaculately shined. His clothes and his determined, resolute demeanour indicated a man who was intelligent, brave and gruff when he was confronting the bad guys or adversity of any kind. Added to that was the feeling that he was always swoon-worthy around the ladies.

Two Girls Who Danced
With the Demon of Darkness

Lynton and Jasmine were both affected by all that swoon-worthiness but add to that the fact that his horizontal yellow-grey eyes were glaring at them like he was examining every centremetre of their sensual bodies, which actually made them tingle just a bit with appreciation for his glare. As the motif of his thickish eyebrows rose outward from twin creases above a hooked nose, and his pale brown hair grew down from high flat temples in a point on his forehead while he looked rather pleasantly upon the two, put them in complete awe.

One truly got an intense sense that this man was cunning, unbeatable in a fistfight and mistrustful of almost everyone. He had little respect for the authorities and was willing to bend the law to get to the truth, but his desire for justice and commitment to a personal code of ethics outweighed any other concern, including love or money. In fact, he reminded both women of the man immortalized by author Wayne Frye, Aaron Adams.

As the waiter put down Spade's coffee, he waited until he was out of earshot to say, "You ladies are treading in dangerous territory. You must be extremely careful. I have held in my hands the stuff that dreams are made of. That Maltese Falcon was an object that wrecked havoc on all who came in contact with it. I am telling you to be leery of this Nick Beale. He is not what he appears to be. Hey, even I might not be whom I appear to be."

Two Girls Who Danced
With the Demon of Darkness

Lynton, leaning slightly toward Spade replied, "Oh, you are exactly whom you appear to be. That is one thing about Sam Spade. What you see is what you get, and thanks for the warning, but we have gone too far now to turn back."

"I expected a reply like that, because I sized you two up as being different from the minute I was told about you by Hercule Poirot. You aren't like the norm. You're not even close. You may occasionally dress yourself up as one of the crowd; even participate in some of the mindless banality of those who are distracted by multi-millionaire sports figures prancing round like they are actually doing something important or celebrities who have to dance around half naked because they lack the talent to generate interest without gimmicks. But it is obvious neither of you care about fitting in. You are appalled by watching so called normal people as they go about their automatic existences trying to emulate those who are contributing nothing positive. You two, no doubt, avoid the clichés of saying things like 'have a nice day' because you know how meaningless it is and that there is no sincerity behind it in a society that teaches superficiality to everyone. You want to talk to people, not ignore them, because you wonder what you might learn from taking a chance on conversation with a complete stranger. Everyone carries a piece of life's puzzle without even realizing it, and you both know that. Nobody comes into your life by mere coincidence. Life is a gamble every time you get out of bed in the morning and you two also know that, which is why I trust your instincts to do the unexpected."

Jasmine chimed in, "Thanks for the praise. We appreciate it, and we will heed your warning when we visit Nick Beale today."

Sighing as he sipped his coffee, Spade then placed his cup down with a distinctive thud and replied, "See that you do that. As I told Brigit O'Shaughnessy in the Case of the Maltese Falcon, 'You won't need much of anybody's help. You're good. Chiefly your eyes, I think, and that throb you get in your voice.' I really enjoy conversing with you two, and I must say also looking at you two while doing so, but I must go."

*Sam Spade
leaving
the café*

*Image
©1941
Warner
Brothers*

Two Girls Who Danced
With the Demon of Darkness

He got up with the same determination with which he had sat down. Most notable was his apparently detached demeanour that you just knew was more act than reality. He had a keen eye for every detail in any room where he was. At six feet tall, he had steep rounded and sloped shoulders which made his body seem almost conical, no broader than it was thick. He actually looked like Humphrey Bogart in his prime. Maybe Dashiell Hammett had Bogart in mind when he wrote *The Maltese Falcon* and *The Big Sleep*. He wasn't handsome, but he had a certain presence about him that made all the ladies in the room swoon as he walked out of the restaurant, Lynton and Jasmine included.

Just as Sam Spade was walking out, he was greeted with a knowing grin and a nod of the head at the door by a chubby elderly woman, who one just instinctively knew was a spinster and a very natural busybody. She had the demeanour of a clever fox and one intuitively knew she was as observant as a hawk in the sky scanning for prey. She looked uninterested in the surroundings, but somehow you just knew that nothing passed her way without her observational acuity analyzing it. It was obvious that strange and exciting events often surrounded her. In fact, she was a magnet for mystery. You just knew it.

Jasmine and Lynton looked at her with total awe. They instinctively knew who she was, even though they both comprehended that she was a fictional character come to life. When she walked to their table and started to introduce herself, Lynton immediately stood up, extended her right hand and blurted out before the woman could utter a word, "Jane Marple."

"Indeed I am," she replied and asked if she could take a seat at the table.

"Of course, please do. We would be delighted." Replied Lynton as Jasmine sat silent and dumbfounded.

"I have heard much about you ladies," offered Miss Marple. "You are about to go up against a monstrous evil, and you need to be prepared. For example, I have heard that you already danced with the evil one in the square here."

"You mean Nick Beale," said Jasmine.

"I do, indeed. He is a wily one. You must be eternally vigilant when around him, and expect the unexpected, because he has more tricks up his sleeve than a Las Vegas magician."

The waiter came over and asked if he could get her anything. She looked up, smiled and said, "Some tea, please."

The waiter left and as they waited his return, Miss Marple sat quietly complementing on the efforts the two had made over the years in the quest for justice. Then, when the waiter brought her tea, she said, "In recording from time to time some of the curious experiences and interesting recollections of my many adventures, I have faced few adversaries more cunning than Mr. Beale, so be very careful when dealing with him. He is a wily one.

Two Girls Who Danced
With the Demon of Darkness

She sipped her tea delicately and after finishing it, slowly rose, pushing her thick frame up almost laboriously. She said something that would stick with the girls: "Remember that there is nothing to be gained by foolish heroism. I know you two have an aversion to publicity. To your sombre and cynical spirits all popular applause has always been abhorrent, and nothing amuses you more at the end of a successful case than to hand over the actual exposure to some orthodox official, and to listen with a mocking smile to the general chorus of misplaced congratulations. This may be a case in which such anonymity is preferred, because few will believe what you are about to encounter. Good luck!"

She waddled out of the dining room toward the stairs, as the two girls looked at her, then one another in complete bewilderment at all the remarkable people they had met. Had they been real, or just imaginary images called up from furtive minds. No, they had to be real. It was obvious, because they had interacted right there in the restaurant with others.

It was then that these two's iron constitutions showed some symptoms of giving way in the face of constant hard work of a most exacting kind pursuing the machinations as a result of the antique phone fascination. They got up and left the restaurant, and on the way back to Jasmine's apartment, which stood high above the square, looking down upon the whole sinister semicircle below, with its placid sheltered shops and apartments, seemed to be inviting the downtrodden of society to meander about in search of something, but what no one could actually decipher.

Ascending the steps to Jasmine's apartment, they turned suddenly and looked back behind them as a sudden swirling round of wind, a blistering gale from the south-west swept all about the square. In every direction there were traces of some vanished hope contained in the curious raging wind which hinted continuing strife was building. The intriguing mystery of the place, with its sinister atmosphere, added to the feeling of doom suddenly overwhelming the two.

In that land of lost dreams, like so many other places in a world ruled by the greedy, where the poor are expected to accept their fate, these two were about to be plunged into a situation which would be more intense, more engrossing, and infinitely more mysterious than any of those with which they were previously occupied. They were about to be precipitated into the midst of a series of events which would cause the utmost excitement and concern in the ancient city of Casablanca.

The place where they stood in observational awe was a small section of a decaying area of Old City that included the cottages and apartments of a couple of thousand inhabitants clustered about an ancient mosque. It was outside that Mosque where the two ladies were walking hurriedly, returning to Nick Beale's home that the Imam of the Mosque,

Two Girls Who Danced
With the Demon of Darkness

Mohammad Yusuf, was, by chance, just leaving the holy structure when, noticing the two ladies, he greeted them in a surprising manner. "My, you two are surely in a hurry. Be careful you are not in a hurry to meet Satan."

This Imam was something of an amateur archaeologist, as Jasmine had made his acquaintance previously while attending an archaeological lecture at the library near where she lived. He was a middle-aged man, portly and affable, with considerable knowledge of local lore. Jasmine and Lynton were not overly alarmed by his comment, but their interest was piqued.

Jasmine introduced Lynton, and he invited them into his dried adobe home next to the Mosque to which Jasmine, grabbing Lynton's arm, for some reason, wanted to accept. Lynton, despite desiring to get to Nick Beale's, assumed there must be a good reason for Jasmine's acceptance.

At his invitation, they took tea and also met Mr. Amid Hassan, an independent gentleman, who increased the clergyman's scanty resources by taking rooms in his large, straggling house. The Imam, being a bachelor, was glad to come to such an arrangement, though he had little in common with his lodger, who was a thin, dark, spectacled man, with a pronounced stoop which gave the impression of actual, physical deformity. The two found the Imam garrulous, but his lodger strangely reticent, a sad-faced, introspective man, sitting with averted eyes, brooding apparently upon his own affairs.

Two Girls Who Danced
With the Demon of Darkness

I mention here these two men, because they will become relevant latter as this mystery unfolds. After tea, the two ladies left, and Lynton immediately asked of Jasmine, "Why did you stop to visit the Imam?"

"This is a Muslin country dear, and it is never wise to ignore an invitation for tea or coffee from an Imam. Anyway, his statement indicated he might be aware of what we are up to, and we might, in the future, need his assistance in some way or another."

"Point understood," replied Lynton.

It was at this time, as they were walking to Beale's home, they suddenly heard footsteps behind them as they turned toward Gloom Way. They both sensed the person behind them and together they halted their steps and quickly turned to face the person.

Having felt obligated by her husband to read the Michael Shayne mysteries, Lynton immediately recognized the red haired detective from the books. There he was, leaning now against a wall.

Mike Shayne ©20th Century Fox

Two Girls Who Danced
With the Demon of Darkness

"You ladies are about to take on a monumental mystery of gigantic proportions," he offered as he lit his pipe.

Lynton, wanting to let him know she knew who he was said, "Yes, Mr. Shayne, we are aware of that."

"Let me give you a little piece of advice ladies. Never let your guard down, because this Mr. Beale is a devious individual who is renowned for his manipulative wiliness. Also, don't expect conventional weapons to work in combating him. He is not subject to any normal rules of engagement. I now bid your adieu and wish you luck."

They nodded their heads, and turned when they heard a commotion on the street above them. It was just an old man pushing a cart. They turned back to address Michael Shayne and he was gone, seemingly disappearing into thin air.

The two of them eventually made it to the Beale house, and as they stood there contemplating their next move, a man, despite the hot weather, wearing a trench coat, stepped beside them and said, "Contemplating what to do next are you?"

Both women recognized him as Detective Columbo, as both had seen him on reruns of the famous television series. Still, they were both shocked at how many old time private eyes had popped up as they pursued the mystery that was perplexing them. All somehow were related to that abominable phone that Jasmine had bought in the antique shop.

Two Girls Who Danced
With the Demon of Darkness

Columbo © Universal Television

He eased over to nearby steps and indicated the ladies should move along with him. He, with dishevelled hair, wrinkled clothes and a cigar in his mouth pointed to the step upon which he was sitting, indicating they should take a seat as he was about to pontificate.

He pointed to Nick Beale's house and said, "That is where forty years ago a memorable birth took place. People around here recall weird noises emanating from the home and all the dogs in the area barked persistently throughout the night of the birth. Less worthy of notice was the fact that the mother of this child was a woman of dubious character known for her decadence, but rarely seen except for her sojourns to pick up men to go back to her house, where some told of unusual sexual acts taking place that were often disgusting in nature. She was a somewhat deformed, unattractive albino woman of perhaps 35, living

with an aged and half-insane father about whom
the most frightful tales of wizardry had been
whispered about in the community. The woman
had no known husband, but made no apologies for
having a child without benefit of marriage. In fact,
there were those who suspected that the child was
a result of an incestuous relationship with her
father. The woman seemed immensely proud of
the dark, but terribly handsome infant that was
rarely seen, but who formed a distinct contrast to
her own sickly and pink-eyed albinism, and there
were mutterings of many curious prophecies about
her newborn son's unusual powers."

"This albino woman, whose name was Lidia,
was a lone creature given to wandering
mysteriously amidst violent storms in the area and
trying to read the great voluminous books which
her father had inherited, and which were fast
falling to pieces with age. She had never been to
school, but was filled with disjointed scraps of
ancient lore that were taught her by her father who
was rarely seen about the Old Quarter. The house
had become feared by all because of her father's
reputation for black magic, and the unexplained
death by violence of his wife when Lidia was
twelve years old. Isolated among strange
influences, Lidia was fond of wild and grandiose
daydreams and singular flights of fancy when she
would mutter strangely to herself. She obviously
had plenty of time for leisure as there were no
standards of order and cleanliness in regards to
maintaining the home."

Two Girls Who Danced
With the Demon of Darkness

Fascinated by Columbo's tale, the two women sat spellbound as he continued. "There was a litany of hideous noises which echoed from and around the house with the dogs in the area often barking furiously. The people in the area also found it unusual that on the night Lidia's son Nick was born no known doctor or midwife presided at his coming since they all feared going to the home. Actually, neighbours knew nothing of Nick until a week afterward, when Lidia's father, Belem, walked to the general store and discoursed incoherently to the group of loungers there. There seemed to be a change in the old man, an added element of furtiveness in the clouded brain which subtly transformed him from an object of pity to an object of fear. Amidst it all he showed some trace of the pride noticed in his daughter. He told the assemblage at the general store the he didn't care what folks thought of Lidia's boy. He said that Lidia was a smart girl, so the boy would be smart, too. He told them she had seen some things that most of them would be afraid to even look at."

"The only persons who saw Nick during the first month of his life were two villagers that had always been friendly with the family, old Demitri Siede and local well-known prostitute, Fatima Hafsa. Fatima's visit was frankly one of curiosity, and her subsequent tales did justice to her observations; but Demitri came to sell some eggs and meat to the family every two weeks. This marked the beginning of a course of meat buying on the part of the family which included purchasing enough beef to feed a small army on a regular basis."

"There came a period when people were curious about the huge amounts of beef being delivered to the residence. It seemed impossible for only three people to eat the huge amount of beef which was being delivered. Then, something else strange cropped up. In the spring after Nick's birth, Lidia resumed her customary rambles, bearing in her miss-proportioned arms the swarthy child. Public interest in the family subsided after most of the townsfolk had seen the baby, and no one bothered to comment on the swift development which that newcomer seemed every day to exhibit. Nick's growth was indeed phenomenal, for within three months of his birth he had attained a size and muscular power not usually found in infants under a full year of age. His motions and even his vocal sounds showed a deliberateness highly peculiar in an infant, and at seven months, he began to walk unassisted, with some faltering, which another month was sufficient to remove. It was somewhat after this time that a great blaze was seen in the top floor window, a dashing fire like light that bounced around the room in an undulating fashion that was accompanied by a wild incantation that could be faintly heard."

Fascination had taken hold of our two heroines and they hung on every word Columbo was uttering. "Considerable talk was started when a man named Ahmed Ali mentioned having seen

Two Girls Who Danced
With the Demon of Darkness

Nick prancing around upstairs in the home late in the evenings. He also saw a bunch of other people in some kind of ritual looking dance. All were entirely unclothed. He could not be sure about the boy, who may have had some kind of a fringed belt and a pair of dark blue trunks or trousers on. Nick was never subsequently seen without complete and tightly buttoned attire, the disarrangement or threatened disarrangement of which always seemed to fill him with anger and alarm. His contrast with his squalid mother and grandfather in this respect was thought very notable until true horror took hold. The next January gossips were mildly interested in the fact that Nick had commenced to talk, and at the age of only eleven months. His speech was somewhat remarkable both because of its difference from the ordinary accents of the region, and because it displayed a freedom from infantile lisping of which many children of three or four might well be proud. The boy was not talkative, yet when he spoke he seemed to reflect some elusive element wholly not possessed by others. The strangeness did not reside in what he said, or even in the simple idioms he used; but seemed vaguely linked with his intonation of the spoken sounds. His facial aspect, too, was remarkable for its maturity as his large, dark eyes gave him an air of quasi-adulthood and well-nigh preternatural intelligence. He was, exceedingly handsome. However, there was something almost goatish or animalistic about his general manner. He was soon disliked even more decidedly than his mother and grandfather. Dogs abhorred the boy, and he was always obliged to take various defensive measures against their barking menace."

It was at this point that Jasmine interjected, "We have danced with him down in the square. He is handsome, but in a sort of devilish way, a way that is frightening."

"Yes, many who know him say that, but let me continue my story. The family continued to consume huge amounts of beef and began a restoration of the abandoned upper story of the house, with the grandfather doing all the work. His mania showed itself only in his tight boarding-up of all the windows in the reclaimed section. Less inexplicable was his fitting-up of another downstairs room for his new grandson, a room which several callers saw, though no one was ever admitted to the closely-boarded upper story. This chamber he lined with tall, firm shelving; along which he began gradually to arrange, in apparently careful order, all the rotting ancient books and parts of books. While all this was going on, obviously the boy grew and when he was 18 months old his size and accomplishments were almost alarming. He had grown as large as a child of four, and was a fluent and incredibly intelligent talker. He ran freely about the area, and accompanied his mother on all her wanderings. At home he would pore diligently over the queer pictures and charts in his grandfather's books. By this time the restoration of the house was finished, and those who watched it wondered why one of the upper windows had been made into a solid plank door. It was a window in the rear of the east gable end, close against the nearby hillside; and no one could imagine why a cleated wooden runway was built up to it from the ground. About the period of this work's completion, people noticed that the old tool-house at the side of the home was tightly locked and the windows boarded up. There also was an unusual odour, a disgusting stench coming from that building."

Lynton and Jasmine were astounded by all that Columbo was sharing, and there fascination showed in their abject attention as he continued. "The following months were void of visible events, save that everyone swore to a slow but steady increase in the mysterious noises from inside the house. Nick was growing up uncannily, so that he looked like a boy of ten as he entered his fourth year. He read avidly by himself now; but talked much less than formerly. A settled taciturnity was absorbing him, and for the first time people began to speak specifically of the dawning look of evil in his ghoulish glare. He would sometimes mutter an unfamiliar jargon that no one was familiar with and chant in bizarre rhythms which chilled the listener with a sense of unexplainable terror. The aversion displayed toward him by dogs had now become a matter of wide remark. The very few callers at the house would often find Lidia alone on the ground floor, while odd cries and footsteps resounded in the boarded-up second story. She would never tell what her father and the boy were doing up there. When the boy was twenty, his precociousness became more pronounced as rumours of black magic being performed in the house became prevalent. For a long while, the tales of goings on at that house began to sink indistinguishably into the general life of a morbid community used to their queer ways and hardened to their eccentricities. Thus ladies are the tales of Nick Beale and his grandfather and mother. Be very leery when you go into that place. You cannot be too careful."

Alarmed, but unafraid, Jasmine and Lynton rose, turned with their backs to Columbo and looked up at the house above them with a growing consternation. They turned to look back at Columbo, and like all the other people who had mysteriously showed up unexpectedly, he had simply disappeared. Still, they were determined to explore the Nick Beale mystery.

The two ladies took a deep breath and stood in awe as they stared at the perplexing house just above them. They were extremely eager to go into the house, but they could not get their timid legs to move. They bewilderingly looked at each other, eyes ablaze with curiosity and determination. Neither of them was known for ever backing down from a challenge, and they both knew this was definitely going to be a challenge of monumental proportions.

CHAPTER 6
Evil of the Foulest Kind

Once, early in the morning, Beelzebub arose,
With care his evil person adorning.
He put on his Sunday clothes.
He drew on boots to hide his hoofs.
He drew on gloves to hide his claws.
His horns were concealed by a fedora,
And the devil went forth as a dandy.

The house the ladies were looking at lived under constant shadow, as if the sun kept reaching for the walls that shrunk away. And so its windows stayed black without the rippling effect of the light, never knowing that the dust of evil clings. The dirt of years could so easily be washed away

Two Girls Who Danced
With the Demon of Darkness

but not the dust of evil. The walls, you could tell, were cold to the touch, stealing the heat from warm fingers. That there were ghouls inside was an almost certainty. That they blustered around screaming was a fact since they had been heard for years. This was an evil place.

Still, the two women were about 100 metres from the house when they saw a familiar person walking toward them. It was none other than famous private eye, Jim Rockford.

Jim Rockford ©Universal Television

Two Girls Who Danced
With the Demon of Darkness

"You ladies look a bit squeamish. You having reservations about knocking on Nick Beale's door?"

Surprised, because she knew James Garner, who played Rockford on television was dead, Jasmine said, "No, but we are surprised to see you here."

"Why would you be surprised? After all, once a P.I., always a P.I."

Not wanting to remind him he was dead, Lynton avoided the obvious and said, "Why are you here? Thought you were strictly a Malibu private eye?"

"Alas ladies, I was summoned here by my friend you know from the phone, Hercule Poirot."

Jasmine said, "So, you know of my purchase that has caused us so much trouble?"

"Of course. It is a purchase you could live to regret or maybe it is purchase that will end a long mystery here in the Old City, a purchase that will make you even greater legends than you already are. I am here to tell you more of the horror of that house (he pointed at the Nick Beale home) over there, a house harbouring evil of the foulest kind."

Taking a seat on the steps, the two ladies looked up at him as he leaned on the hand railing and began his tale. "In the course of time, callers professed to hear sounds in the sealed upper story, even when all the family were downstairs, and they wondered how swiftly or how lingeringly a family could consume so much beef. There was talk of a complaint to the Society for the Prevention of Cruelty to Animals; but nothing ever came of it, since Old City folk are never anxious to call the outside world's attention to themselves. When Nick was a boy of ten whose mind, voice, stature, and bearded face gave all the impressions of maturity, a second great siege of carpentry went on at the house. It was all inside the sealed upper part, and from bits of discarded lumber people concluded that the youth and his grandfather had knocked out all the partitions and even removed the attic floor, leaving only one vast open void between the ground story and the peaked roof."

Jim Rockford eased onto a step, taking a seat. "One night, the old grandfather lay dying and a doctor was called. He found the old man in a very grave state, with a cardiac action and torturous breathing that told of an end not far off. The daughter and Nick stood by the bedside, while from the vacant abyss overhead there came a disquieting suggestion of rhythmical surging or lapping, as of the waves on some level beach. The doctor, though, was chiefly disturbed by the chattering night birds outside; a seemingly limitless legion of whippoorwills that cried their endless message in repetitions timed diabolically to the wheezing gasps of the dying man. It was uncanny and unnatural. Toward one o'clock the old man gained consciousness, and interrupted his wheezing to choke out a few words to his grandson. It was the same for more than an hour, when the final throaty rattle came."

Jim took a deep breath and continued, "Nick Beale, as time passed after his grandfather's death,

Two Girls Who Danced
With the Demon of Darkness

became a recognized scholar of really tremendous erudition in his one-sided way, and was quietly known by correspondence to many librarians in distant places where rare and forbidden books of old days were kept. He was more and more hated and dreaded around the Old Quarter because of certain youthful female disappearances which suspicion laid vaguely at his door; but was always able to silence inquiry through fear over the years, Nick had treated his albino mother with a growing contempt. It became obvious to all that she was afraid of him, and then one day she just disappeared and was never seen again. Carrying a valise, this miscreant young man went in search of something called the *Necronomicon* as printed in Spain in the Seventeenth Century. There was a copy of it **at** King Abdul-Aziz Al Saoud Foundation's Library in the city. In the reference section, locked away in a special section of the library, he was given access to the book. He at once began searching for a certain passage as he was looking, he had to admit, for a kind of formula or incantation containing the frightful name *Yog-Sothoth*, and it puzzled him to find discrepancies, duplications, and ambiguities which made the matter of determination far from easy. As he copied the formula, he finally found it also contained a notation that man is either the oldest or the last of earth's masters. It stated that the *Old Ones* were, are and shall be not in the spaces we know, but between them. It said that they walked determined, serene and primal, un-dimensioned and unseen. It said that *Yog-Sothoth* was the gate keeper. Past, present, future, all are one in *Yog-Sothoth*. He knows where the *Old Ones* once broke through, and where they shall break through again and they can only be identified by their foul smell as they walk. Man rules now where they ruled once, but they are hungry to regain their power. Nick Beale was going to be a conduit for that power and had committed the murder of his own mother in the process of gaining that power."

Realizing that Nick Beale might have committed matricide, the two women felt a wave of fright as tangible as a draft of a tomb's cold clamminess. The man, with whom they had once danced, seemed like the spawn of another planet or dimension; like something only partly of mankind and linked to blackness of the foulest kind. The two women looked at one another in quizzical amazement. Then, they turned to look at Jim Rockford, who they assumed would go on with more of his tale. No, he would not go on, as like all the others, he had simply disappeared.

Not surprised by the sudden turn of events, they made their way toward Nick Beale's house once again. On their way, coming down the steps was another private eye. This one Lynton immediately recognized and turned to Jasmine and said, "Here we go again."

Looking directly at the man descending the cobblestone stairs, Jasmine said, "Okay, another well-known private eye."

"Right!" replied Lynton.

Two Girls Who Danced
With the Demon of Darkness

The man, with sleepy, droopy eyes nodded his head and said, "Good day, Ladies."

Lynton turned to Jasmine and said, "Meet Mr. Philip Marlowe, Jasmine."

Philip Marlowe
© RKO Radio
Pictures

At this time, Lynton was thankful for all the old movies her husband had made her watch, as she was well-prepared for all the sleuths who were showing up in Casablanca.

Marlow, in his customary sarcastic tone, said, "Ah, always good to be known."

Lynton quoted Marlow from Raymond Chandler's *Murder My Sweet*, "Okay Marlowe, I said to myself. You're a tough guy. You've been sapped twice, choked, beaten silly with a gun, shot in the arm until you're crazy as a couple of waltzing mice. Now let's see you do something really tough - like putting your pants on."

"Ah, you have read *Murder My Sweet*."

"Seen the movie."

Grinning his sarcastic smile, he replied, "Easier than reading I suppose."

"Indubitably," offered Lynton.

Like his predecessor, Marlowe sat on the steps and pointed for the girls to take a seat by him.

The girls were getting used to listening to stories from famous private eyes, so they leaned forward and got ready for another tale. "Let me tell you

Two Girls Who Danced
With the Demon of Darkness

about my first experience and the strange goings on at 111 Gloom Way. What I saw there is enough to jangle the nerves of the most ardently stern individual. In fact, Ms. Viñas, even someone like you, who is famous for dealing with demons, would have been frightened by what happened."

The eyes of our two heroines gazed with solemn expectation into the face of Marlowe, who seemed to gather awe from the recollections he was summoning. The cobblestone steps were a good scene for such a narrative, within which you might imagine what shadows you please.

Marlowe cleared his voice, rolled his eyes slowly round, and began his tale. "I was new to Casablanca the night I came to the house up there. My aunt was the housekeeper, and I was going to spend the summer with her when I was a small boy. I was a bit frightened, and when I saw the eerie looking house, I wished myself back again with my mother. I was immediately told to never go upstairs, as no one but the Beale's were allowed up there."

"It's a shame to frighten a poor foolish child like I was. And whenever I told people where I was staying they got a queer look on their faces, and I was told by several people that the devil dwelled there. The house was the most frightening thing I had ever seen. A great white-and-black house with great beams across and right up it, and gables looking out, as white as a sheet, to the moon, and the shadows on the trees, two or three up and down in front, you could easily count the leaves on them, and all the little diamond-shaped window-panes, glimmering on the great windows, and shutters, old fashioned, hinged on the wall outside, bolted across all the rest of the windows in front. All these were maintained by the three or four servants who were mostly there days only except for my aunt, and the albino lady in the house, and the boy and old man. Most of the rooms were locked up."

Marlow shifted his position, stretching out his legs. "My dear aunt brought me to her rather austere room. She was tall and thin, with a pale face and black eyes, and long thin hands which she kept black mittens on all the time. She was past fifty, and her word was short; but her word she made plain to me was law. I have no complaints to make of her; but she was a hard woman when it came to discipline. I know there were rumours of ill treatment of the albino woman, but I have to say what I saw indicated she was well taken care of, although it might have been because of my aunt, who had a conscience and was a compassionate person. She had fine wages, but she was a bit stingy, and kept all her fine clothes under lock and key, and wore, mostly, dark cotton full body aprons. I had my own little alcove within her bedroom and the bath was just down the hall."

Lynton and Jasmine were getting a bit bored with the detailed descriptions, but elected to abstain from interrupting, as they did not want to disturb his train of thought. He continued his tale.

Two Girls Who Danced
With the Demon of Darkness

"When I went into the adjacent room, there was tea on the table and an elaborate cake. There was a Mrs. Vern, who was fat, jolly and very talkative. In fact, she said more in an hour than my aunt would in a year. While I was having tea with Mrs. Vern, my aunt went to see the albino woman, Lidia."

"After awhile visiting with Mrs. Vern, my aunt came to retrieve me and took me aside to say that I should be leery of Mrs. Vern as she was a troublesome old lady who talked too much, but likened it to her age, which I was surprised to find out was 83, which seemed a bit old to still be working, but the poor often have no choice in a world where the few get plenty and the rest of us get leftovers. Anyway, my aunt told me to be nice to her. She then told me that Mrs. Vern was terribly upset when a young girl named Lilly had worked there for awhile, but one day just didn't show up for work, and no one ever knew what happened to her, as even her parents said she didn't return home from work one day and they never heard from her again. Over time, I began to feel more comfortable and at home. Once when I was walking about the room looking' at this thing and at that I became particularly interested in pretty old china things on the cupboard, and pictures again the wall; and there was a door open across the hallway, and I saw a queer old leathern jacket with straps and buckles to it, and sleeves as long as the bed-post hanging on a hook inside the room near the door."

Two Girls Who Danced
With the Demon of Darkness

Taking a deep breath, Marlowe continued, "Mrs. Vern was sitting in the room rocking away and my aunt walked in and asked me what I had in my hand. Turning about, I said that I didn't know what it was. Pale as she was, the red came up in her cheeks, and her eyes flashed with anger, and I think she had half a dozen steps to take, until she grabbed my shoulders and shook me, and she plucked the thing out of my hand, telling me not to be handling things like the expensive china. I looked over at Mrs. Vern with tears in my eyes, and I could see sympathy for me resonating in her demeanour, which made me feel close to her. She told my aunt not to be so hard on me as I meant no harm. I was instructed to go to bed. Mrs. Vern walked out, leaving the house for the day. I went to my bed. I lay for a while awake and heard whisperings coming from where my aunt was, but I assumed she must be talking to herself as everyone had left the house except for the Beale's and my aunt and me.

Seeing the ladies were getting impatient with his tale, Marlowe said, "Be patient. I am getting to the point directly. The next day my aunt sent me out for a walk. I was glad when I came back. The trees were so big, and the place so dark and lonesome, and it was a cloudy day, and I cried a bit, thinking of home, while I was walking alone there. That evening, I was sitting in my room, and the curtain was open into my aunt's chamber. It was, then, for the first time I heard what I suppose was someone talking I assumed to my aunt. It was a queer noise more than talking. I pricked my ears to hear all I could, but I could not make out one word that was said from the other party in the room with my aunt. However, I did very distinctly hear my aunt say that the evil one could hurt no one without Lidia's approval."

"I kept listening with my ear turned to curtain that separated my room, holding my breath, but not another word or sound came in. In about twenty minutes, as I was sitting by the table, looking at the pictures in a book of *Aesop's Fables*, I was aware of something moving at the curtain separating the rooms on the outside, and looking up I saw my aunt's face looking in where the curtains were drawn together. She separated them and whispered to me that she would be right back, as she needed to check on the Beale's. She left me alone wondering who that low voice belonged to."

Marlowe seemed more determined in his voice now. "I kept looking at the book as before, still listening every now and then, but there was no sound, not a breath that I could hear, but I felt someone was still there. I began whispering to the pictures and talking to myself to keep my heart up, for I was growing deathly afraid there alone, assuming someone was still in the other part of the large room. At last up I got and began walking about my part of the room, looking at this and peeping at that, to amuse my mind, until I finally mustered enough nerve to very discreetly open the curtain separating my part of the room."

Two Girls Who Danced
With the Demon of Darkness

"I finally got enough nerve to separate the curtains and walked into the outer part of the room on tiptoe, and looked around. Then I took a peek at myself in the big mirror on the far wall. I could see the fear in my face. And there was something else. I could see the reflection in the mirror of someone lying on my aunt's bed."

"There she was, dressed out. Satin and silk, and scarlet and green, and gold and pint lace. What a sight, even for a young boy. Despite all that I was intensely frightened. Still, I couldn't take my eyes off her; my very heart stood still. And in an instant she opens her eyes and up she sits, and spins herself around, stands up and stares right in my face with her two great glassy eyes, and a wicked smile slowly creeps across her thick, succulent lips. Still, she seemed more dead than alive. I was so scared. She put her fingers straight out pointing at me, and said in a very creepy voice, 'I killed the boy? So what? That's just what I do. That's the power of Marie Laveau.' I tell you I have never been so crept out in my life."

Jasmine and Lynton had met a woman named Marie Laveau in that very house. How could it be the same woman, because the one they saw was in her twenties? She could not have been the same woman described by Marlowe.

Marlowe took a deep breath and continued with his story, "Yes, that is the same woman you met, despite the fact she has never seemed to age. Do not doubt her powers. When I saw her if I'd thought for an instant, I'd a turned about and run.

Two Girls Who Danced
With the Demon of Darkness

But I couldn't take my eyes off her, and I backed from her as soon as I could; and she came clattering toward me like a thing on wires, with her fingers pointing to my throat. I kept backing and backing as quickly as I could, and her fingers were only a few inches away from my throat, and I felt I'd lose my wits if she touched me. I went back right into the corner, and I gave a blood curdling yell and that minute my aunt calls out and Laveau turns about and ran from the room down the hallway. I cried heartily and threw my arms around my aunt. My aunt reached out and embraced me as I sobbed and sobbed. She told me not to be afraid that it was just a crazy woman who was related to the Beale family and she lived in the basement, and it was best if I never went there as she should not be disturbed as she had been crazy ever since her husband died. I told her about what she said in regards to killing a boy and my aunt said that I should not worry since the woman was not right in the head. She had married a member of the family who was a widower who had a son about nine years old. It seems this woman was rarely seen as she was a recluse. The man died a few months after the marriage and the young boy fell under the care of his stepmother. There never were more tales of this boy after one morning. No one could say where he went. The only sign of him was his hat which was found on the beach near here. It was thought he apparently drowned. It was said the step-mother, Marie Laveau, knew more than she was telling. Now, one might think that is the end of the story but it is not."

Jasmine and Lynton's interest was now piqued to a feverish pitch, since they had met a woman named Marie Laveau the night they also met Nick Beale. Still, it could not be the same woman, as the individual they met was in her twenties. But……

Marlowe continued. "Now. I am going to tell you about what I saw with my own eyes. I was very nervous during my sojourn there, but being a typical child, my interest in Marie Laveau simply made me even more curious about what was going on. There was a huge room right at the foot of the stairs in the basement. The walls of that room were covered with thick panels except on one side of the room was an area that had the panels removed and brick had been used to cover that area of the wall. Opposite that wall was a huge mirror. One night I got restless and slipped out of my room without my aunt's knowledge. I went down the stairs to that huge room by the foot of the stairs. What a strange feeling I had when I heard the grandfather clock in the hallway above the basement stairs strike twelve as I had the desire to creep into that abominable room. I eased into it and my back was turned to the door and my eyes toward the wall where the bricks were. It was then that I saw a light flickering through the bricks on the wall before me, as if something took fire behind them, and a weird undulating shadow began dancing around the room. This small, childlike shadow was dancing up and down on the ceiling beams and the panels; and I turned my head over my shoulder quickly, thinking something must be on fire. What did I see in the mirror on that far wall but the image of a little boy. There was a red light that rose above the image of the boy and suddenly he started moving toward me. He passed me by, with a blast of cold air, and his little hands seemed to be searching for something over in the far corner. He turned around to me, like a thing on a pivot. All at once the room was completely dark, and I was just standing there dumbfounded. As you might guess, I ran out of the room filed with fear. My aunt was up when I raced into the room and held me by the hand, and looked hard in my face all the time. And she told me not to be afraid, but to tell her what happened, which I did. She said that she had always suspected foul play in the death of the boy and that Marie Laveau had that wall sealed up by her own hand not long after the boy disappeared. It was then that my aunt packed up my things the next day, and I was sent home to my mother. I had not been back with my mother more than a week when news came that my aunt had died in an accident. Needless to say, my mother and I were devastated when we heard the news. There was no funeral. She was just buried in the Beale family plot the very day she died. No service, no nothing just word she had died in an accident. That was the last we ever heard from the Beale's. It was an affair that preyed on my mind for years."

Perplexed, Lynton asked, "And what was the accident?"

"That is even stranger," offered Marlowe. "She apparently died at the bottom of the basement stairs as she was trying to race up them. The assumption was she was frightened by something and tried to get out of the basement, but tripped going up the stairs and fell to her death, broke her neck in the fall."

Lynton and Jasmine looked at each other in disbelief. They stood up, as did Marlowe. He pointed at the house, and as the two women were looking at it he said, "There is evil up there, evil of the foulest kind."

The two women stood staring at the house, then turned to address Marlowe. He had disappeared. Not surprised by his disappearance, Lynton uttered his last words: "There is evil up there, evil of the foulest kind."

<u>CHAPTER 7</u>
Foster Fear

He sat them down in Casablanca town,
Before earth's morning ray;
With them, he began to chat,
On religion, and scandal, this and that,
Until the dawn of day.

The Devil was a manipulative one,
And the two heroines' fear did grow.
Looking over at the two, he grinned,
And winked as if they had sinned,
And were about to confront woe.

Satan to them did not appear small.
One would think that the innocents were fair.
Yet, scared; they just did nothing at all.

Two Girls Who Danced
With the Demon of Darkness

But they knew he was planning an evil ball,
As the he was searching for souls there.

Declared the two, if the Tempter was there,
His presence they would not abide.
For they might have a trick or two
That the righteous could do,
Since they had right on their side.

Thought Satan, I will make evil here thrive.
It will best all the others.
I will capture the dying and dead,
And evil will never go to bed,
For all evil doers are brothers.

Marlowe was gone, and the girl's felt a bit perplexed as to what their next step might be. It was then that coming down the street was none other than world renowned mystery writer and amateur detective, Jessica Fletcher.

Jessica Fletcher
©
CBS Television,
Universal Television
&
Corymore Productions

Two Girls Who Danced
With the Demon of Darkness

Jessica Fletcher was a woman on a mission, as she approached Jasmine and Lynton. In fact, the look of determination on her face belied her usual calm nature.

Perplexed, but since they had been constantly exposed to renowned fictitious sleuths there in Casablanca, Lynton and Jasmine stood, not in awe, but in respect. They waited patiently for Jessica to greet them.

"Jessica Fetcher, ladies. It is a pleasure to meet two such renowned women. You two may be the last chance to tackle an evil that has been incubating here for many years, an evil that has been waiting to unleash itself on an unsuspecting world. There is a death that is going to unleash the forces of darkness as never before. You will think they are unrelated to what is going on (she pointed at Beale's house) up there, but they are not. Be very careful; because there are forces at work here that know no boundaries in the evil about to be unleashed."

She meandered past them as she uttered a name, "Mohammad Yusuf. Remember what I told you – be careful."

She walked down the cobblestone steps of the street, turned to the right and disappeared behind a stucco wall. Not surprising the girls thought, since it appeared all the renowned sleuths they had met somehow managed to disappear into thin air.

Mohammad Yusuf, the imam, was lying dead in the old tower in the Mosque. The body had been discovered, under strange circumstances, and in a place where it might have lain the better part of a week undisturbed; and a dreadful suspicion astounded the people who attended that Mosque as speculation spread rapidly through Old Town

A sunset was glaring through a gorge of the western mountains, turning into fire the twigs of trees, rising with airy lightness from the level sward by the margin of the shadows from the tower of the Mosque, and backed by the grand amphitheatre of the fells at the other side, tinged with the vaporous red of the western light.

Mohammad Yusuf, the Imam, a man of about fifty or upwards, had passed an hour or two with some village cronies the night before his body was discovered. He generally turned in at about nine o'clock most nights and it was assumed he did the same the night he was killed.

Many things were now raked up and talked over about him. In early youth, he had been a bit of a scamp. He ran away from home as a youth. He had gotten into bad scrapes and out again; and, just as the little world of Old Town had come to the conclusion that it would be well for all parties, except, perhaps himself, a happy good riddance for his afflicted mother, if he never returned. However, one day he showed up, a reformed man at the ripe age of forty.

For many, many years he had disappeared, and no one knew what had become of him. Then, suddenly, he reappeared at the Mosque, a very reverent man, sedate and orderly. His mother was dead and buried; but the "prodigal son" was received good-naturedly as it appeared to all that his hardened heart and been softened and he eventually became an Imam serving the Prophet Mohammad and God. It also appeared that he had led a hard life, as he had gotten a good deal of hard muscle. In fact, it was assumed he had been in the military as he stood like a soldier, and the mark over his right eye looked like it came from a gunshot. People wondered how he could have survived a gunshot over the eye, but a pistol bullet from a small calibre weapon often does not penetrate too deep into the area of bone right above the eye. Still, the masses automatically attributed his survival to "God's will."

Nonetheless, regardless of his past, he started out as a Bilal (person who does the call-to-prayer and assists the Imam). He was a punctual Bilal and never failed in his duties. He meddled with no other person's business. He was a fairly silent man, and by no means particularly popular, but he was respected for his devotion to duty. He was reserved in company; and he used to walk alone by the shore of the ocean and in the midst of the general talk was a saturnine listener and showed great compassion. Still, there was something sinister in this man's face; and when things went wrong with him, he could look dangerous. There were whispered stories about his past, but there was no verification of the same. However, there is nothing more mysterious than the spread of rumours. It is like a vial poured on the air. It travels, like an epidemic, on the sightless currents of the atmosphere, or by the laws of a telluric influence equally intangible. These stories treated, though darkly, of the long period of his absence from his native place; but they took no well-defined shape.

On the evening before the tragedy came to light, as trifles are always remembered after the catastrophe, a boy passed him by while he was seated on a bench at the base of a tree in the park across from the Mosque counting silver money. His body and limbs were bent together, his knees were up to his chin, and his long fingers were grasping the money. He glanced at the boy like the devil looking over his next victim.

He had become an Imam when his esteemed predecessor died unexpectedly and he had been in his position for 7 years, and still rumours circulated about him and his past. There was also the boarder, Ahmad Hassan, whose quarters were at the rear of the house. At what time of the night he could not tell, he awoke, and saw a man with his hat on in his room. He had a candle in his hand, which he shaded with his coat from his eye; his back was towards him, and he was rummaging in the drawer in which Ahmad usually kept his money.

He was frightened when she saw the figure in his room, and he could not tell whether his uninvited visitor might not have made his entrance from the contiguous courtyard. So, sitting boldly upright in his bed, demanded: "In God's name, what want you there?"

Two Girls Who Danced
With the Demon of Darkness

"If you only knew," was his reply.

Turning on his heel, he left him. In the morning, Ahmad noticed the Imam was gone. Not only in his lodging was there no account of him, but, when inquiry began to be extended, nowhere in the Old City could he be found.

Still he might have gone off, on business of his own, to some distant village before the town was stirring; and the Imam had no near kindred to trouble their heads about him. People, therefore, were willing to wait and take his disappearance ultimately for granted.

At three o'clock Ahmad, standing at his hall door, looking across the square towards the hills, saw two men approaching across the way in a straight line, apparently coming from the waterfront. They were carrying between them something which, though not very large, seemed ponderous. It was actually a large speaker to broadcast the Adhan (call to prayer).

Ahmad asked then where they got it and one of the men said, "We found it in our boat, where it was left by the Imam we suppose, as it had this Mosque's name on it. So, we brought it here."

Ahmad responded, "We must try to see if there is a speaker missing from the tower."

At this point, Ahmad started getting concerned about the Imam, who had still not returned. He said that he had a key to the Adhan tower where the speaker was located. Leading the way, with his own key in his hand, he turned it in the lock, and stood in the shadows and then shut the door.

Two Girls Who Danced
With the Demon of Darkness

A sack, half full, laid on the ground, with an open end and a piece of cord lying beside it. Something clanked within it as one of the men shoved it aside with the clumsy push of his shoe. The dusky glow from the western sky, entering through a narrow window, illuminated the shafts and arches, the old oak carvings, and the discoloured elements all about, with the melancholy glare of eventide.

The gloom of the tower was obvious as, stooping, the men entered the narrow door that opened at the foot of the winding stair that led to top of the tower; from which a rude ladder-stair of wood had to be pulled down.

Up the narrow stairs the men climbed. It was very dark: a narrow bow-slit in the thick wall admitted the only light they had to guide them. The sparrows in the loft twittered incessantly.

Checking, it was obvious there was no speaker missing, but Ahmad just assumed maybe the Imam had decided on a newer, more powerful one.

"Good gracious!" gasped Ahmad, who, seeing indistinctly a dark mass lying on the floor, had stooped to examine it, and placed his hand upon a cold, dead face. The men drew the body into the streak of light that traversed the floor. It was the corpse of Imam Mohammad Yusuf! There was that frightful scar right above his eye.

The alarm was given and word quickly spread. The police and soon the medical examiner were on the spot; and many curious and horrified spectators of minor importance rushed to the

Two Girls Who Danced
With the Demon of Darkness

scene. Among those rushing to the scene were Jasmine and Lynton. The first thing ascertained was that the man must have been dead for many hours. The next was that his skull was fractured, across the forehead, by an awful blow. The next was that his neck was broken.

His hat was found on the floor, where he had probably laid it, with his handkerchief in it. The sack was examined, and found to contain a silver salver that had disappeared, according to Ahmad Hassan about a month before, the Imam's gold writing case, which he thought he had forgotten somewhere in the Mosque; silver spoons, and various other items, the mysterious disappearance of which spoils had, of late dates, begun to make the honest little community uncomfortable.

The body was carried into the Mosque and laid on a bench and immediately covered with a white sheet; and the townsfolk came grouping in to have a peep at the corpse, and stood around, looking darkly, and talking quietly, mostly in whispers. The conjectures were numerous and many very wild. Meanwhile, Jasmine and Lynton primarily were observers, but they were noticed by Ahmad who gave them a knowing nod.

"What do you think?" said one person to Jasmine.

"The devil will have his due," came an aside from another observer nearby. "That Imam has a very chequered past and just maybe it caught up with him. I have seen some very mysterious going on with that fellow, despite being an Imam."

Two Girls Who Danced
With the Demon of Darkness

"True enough," replied the one who had spoken to Jasmine. "You know there was another person killed just like this one was, a few months ago. Got a slash across the head just like the Imam. Still, this is definitely the devil's work."

Knowing a lot about religion, Lynton interjected, "The devil's supposed to be afraid of churches. I assume the same would apply to Mosques."

One of the men replied, "You got that right little missy, but you just never know. Satan is a wily one. Maybe the tower ain't considered part of the Mosque."

The last tint of sunset was fading from the sky by this time and some were speculating on the motives for what had occurred. Perhaps he had intended to rob the Mosque of donations and had tumbled backwards and broken his neck upon the floor of the loft. After all, no one knew what he had been up to the whole time he was gone. Maybe he had been in prison someone said.

Due to the Adhan speaker and the contents of the sack it was surmised he meant to convey them to the shore and row off and with the help of his spade and pick to bury the proceeds in the forest, return after an absence of but a few hours unmissed and unobserved. He would no doubt, having secured his booty, have made such arrangements as would have made it appear that the Mosque had been broken into. He would, of course, have taken all measures to divert suspicion from himself, and have watched for a suitable opportunity to repossess himself of the buried treasure and dispose of it in safety over a period of time.

And now came out, into sharp relief, all the stories that had one way or other stolen after him into the area. A woman named Mrs. Pullen told the authorities that she thought he was the robber who accosted her one night and stole all her jewellery, but she had not reported her suspicions, thinking it was he who was the robber out of fear she would be ostracized by naming the Imam as the robber. There were the stories also told by a variety of people who had carried a grudge against the Imam.

The evening's fleeting light soon expired, and twilight was succeeded by the early night. Lynton and Jasmine meandered leisurely back to her place to mull over the days events and to make a decision on what should be done about Nick Beale.

A bright moon hung in the frosty sky. The mist rose from the sea had rolled inland. The air was stirless. Through the boughs and sprays of the trees no sigh or motion, however hushed, was audible. Not a ripple glimmered on Old City, which at one point only reflected the brilliant moon from its dark blue expanse like burnished steel. The road that ran by Jasmine's door, along the margin of the square, shone dazzlingly white. White as ghosts, among the dark holly and juniper. The place was quiet by this time. Except for the townsfolk who were now collected in area restaurants, no inhabitant was now outside his or her own threshold.

Jasmine invited Lynton to stay with her. Exhausted, she agreed. Both could not stop thinking of the Imam, and could not get the fixed features of the dead man out of their heads, when they heard the sharp, though distant ring of a person walking on the cobblestone road. It was an unusual walk. More like hoofs than feet. More like someone deliberately making noise in the stillness, a noise to grate on nerves and to foster fear.

**Two Girls Who Danced
With the Demon of Darkness**

CHAPTER 8
What I Saw

The Devil's Song

*The wealthy yeoman, as he wanders
His fertile fields among,
And on his thriving cattle ponders,
Counts his sure gains, and hums a song.
Thus did the Devil, through earth walking,
Hum low a hellish song.*

*For they thrive well whose garb of gore
Is Satan's choicest livery,
And they thrive well who from the poor
Have snatched the bread of penury,
And heap the houseless wanderer's store*

Two Girls Who Danced
With the Demon of Darkness

On the rank pile of luxury.
The leaders thrive, though they are big;
The lawyers thrive, though they are thin;
For every gown, and every wig,
Hides the safe thrift of hell within.
And cormorants are sin-like lean,
And no compassion can be seen.

Sharp instinct apprised Canadian ex-patriot Timothy Dalton of the approach of a guest to the Dragon Inn down the hillside from where Jasmine lived. His experienced ear told him that the person was approaching directly toward the inn, which, after crossing that wide and dismal square, enters the Old City by joining other thoroughfares in front of the Dragon Inn and near the place where the Imam was killed or died by accident.

A clump of tall cypress-like trees stood at this exact point; but the moon shone full upon the winding road and cast its shadow backward. The feet were plainly coming at a rapid pace, with a hollow rattle to them. Timothy wondered how he had heard the sound so well in the frosty night air that hung heavy all about.

He peeked out the window and saw a man. It was someone who resembled Nick Beale, but was it he? No, probably not. He was tall, striding forth with determination. He must have turned the corner of the Imam's house at the moment when Timothy's eyes were wearied; for when Timothy saw him for the first time he was advancing in the hazy moonlight, like the shadow of a cavalier at a gallop upon the level strip of road that skirts the margin of the square upon which the Dragon Inn set.

The hotelier had not very long to wonder why the person rushed at such furious a pace, and how he came to have heard him so far away. A very few moments sufficed to bring the man to the inn door.

The man approached the door and it appeared to almost open by itself as a weird light seemed to form around the man, initiating a dark shadow on the floor. He looked familiar to Timothy, just like Nick Beale. Yet, there was no greeting of familiarity, so Timothy thought it best not to ask if he was Nick Beale. The man, as mentioned previously, was tall like Beale with a sinewy figure. He wore a cape or short mantle, a cocked hat, and a pair of jack-boots, such as held their ground in some primitive cultures where the gentry was always immaculately dressed.

"Don't I know you," asked Timothy Dalton.

The man, his face obscured by the collar of his cloak and his tilted hat replied, "Maybe yes, maybe no."

Strange thought Timothy, but he just let it go. Meanwhile, the man turned and made his way toward the restaurant dining area. And on in he went, as if he had known the place all his days: not seeming to hurry himself, stepping leisurely but gliding on at a steadily rapid rate. He looked like a an athletic man of forty, burned half black by the sun with a pair of fierce black eyes just visible under the edge of his hat; and his mouth seemed divided beneath the moustache he sported. Several people there thought he looked like Nick Beale, but no one dared ask him if he was.

Many of the customers there were discussing their theories about the death of the Imam, when the person who looked like Beale entered. The man lifted his hat slightly, with a sort of smile for a moment. It was then that those there knew it must be Nick Beale. If not, the resemblance was uncanny.

"What do you call this place, gentlemen?" asked the man.

"The Dragon," offered a patron.

"The Dragon," repeated the man, expanding his long hands as he walked nonchalantly about.

Another patron said, "The name is over the door."

"So it is," said the man. "I just wanted to hear someone say it. You know it is said that the devil has dragons in hell to keep the fires going there."

Looks of amazement crossed the faces of all the people there. The kind of amazement that was asking what is this guy up to with his weird questions. Then he offered another interesting observation. "You catch all sorts of worshippers of the devil: courtiers, fanatics, scamps who'll wind up in hell. Everybody is welcome in hell no less. What holiday, fun or fair has got so many pleasant faces together here tonight? When I last called here everyone looked sad then, too. It was on a Friday, the Muslim holy day, that dismalest of holidays; and it would have been positively melancholy only that your Imam, that saint upon earth, was here." He started looking around, over his shoulder, and added: "Ha! Don't see him here?"

Fear grew among those there, as this person seemed genuinely eerie. All gaped in his direction as, with a nod, he turned his eyes and looked toward the far wall.

A patron said, "He's not here. He can't be. He's met an accident of sorts, sir. He's dead."

Upon this the individuals there entertained the stranger with the narrative, which they made easy by a division of labour, two or three generally speaking at a time, and no one being permitted to finish a second sentence without finding himself corrected and supplanted.

"The man's in heaven," someone uttered.

Smiling, the stranger said, "What! He was fiddling with the Mosque speaker was he, and now he is dispatched to heaven? Interesting how everyone is assumed to be in heaven, when in my experience hell is much more crowded than heaven."

The stranger was rubbing those there the wrong way, as he was becoming more irreverent toward religion. A dogmatic patron confronted him directly, "We don't talk against religion here."

"Why not? Have you not all lived with the son of Satan here for a long time now?"

That was a catalyst for those there to realize that the nearly unrecognizable stranger was not a stranger at all, but one Nicholas Beale, a man of mystery who had been the subject of conjecture for years. There was a noticeable pall of fear suddenly descended on all there.

Meanwhile, up the way, Lynton and Jasmine were at her window, looking down across the square at The Dragon where they had followed with their keen eyes the stranger making the foul noises as he trod over the cobblestones.

In very short order, they had systematically determined to make their way to the place where he was now holding court. When they defiantly strolled into The Dragon, the men were as surprised by the presence of women as they were by the stranger, who by now had been openly and categorically identified by Jasmine who said, "Mr. Nick Beale. Surprised to see you. Are you trying to hide who you are?"

"Not I," replied a contemplative Nick. "I came down here from my home where it is pitch black and as rotten as the grave, but to me it is like the love of a mother embracing a new born. And the Imam's death has brightened my day even more, because the death of a religious leader, who grifts off the foolish ones, is to be celebrated not mourned."

All there were surprised and in awe that they were in the presence of the feared and mocked Nick Beale. They began to recognize him now, to comprehend they were in the presence of evil. The talk went on, but Beale grew silent. He seated himself on a bench towards which he extended his feet and hands with seeming enjoyment; his cocked hat still a little over his face.

Lynton and Jasmine were the only females there, and they felt as if proper etiquette had been broached enough as the company began to thin. Two gentlemen near the door were the first to go; then some of the humbler townsfolk. The last bowl of punch was now dry and our heroines moved toward the door, but were surprised when Nick Beale opened it for them and said, "You ladies wanted to talk to me. Perhaps now is the time."

He moved outside The Dragon with them, as Lynton said, "Perhaps. You see, we have been warned about you, but also encouraged to find out what is going on at your place."

"Going on at my place. Just the work of my father. That's all."

"Your father," stated Lynton.

Smiling craftily, Nick replied, "Yes, my beloved father, the prince of so-called evil, whom I am proud to serve. Today, I celebrate the death of one of the earth's worst evils – a religious charlatan, as most religious leaders are. People who spew out assurances to foolish conscripts of their promises of eternal life. I condemn their largesse of real evil – the evil of finger-pointing condemnation which they spew out like water over Victoria Falls."

"I accept your disdain for the charlatans of religion, which unfortunately far outnumber those who are not hypocrites, and I am an avowed atheist, but my belief in the goodness of the majority of humanity makes me think there are a few true believers who actually do not practice hypocrisy, some who see suffering and truly reach out with the hand of compassion," offered Lynton.

A creepy smile eased across Beale's face as he looked directly at Lynton. "Foolish woman. You have too much faith in humanity."

"I probably do, but I have encountered a few genuinely kind people in my 40 years, but I also admit that some of the most cruel have met have proclaimed themselves very religious. It seems far too many proclaiming to be religiously virtuous do not practice what is preached in the Koran and the Bible, although both books are filled with tales of a God who is to often very vengeful and cruel."

Smiling sinisterly, Beale said, "Ah, those are the people tailor-made for darkness eager to recruit people for an eternity in hell."

A man named Amir Assad, wearing a Moroccan Jellaba, walked past the three people outside The Dragon. He greeted the ladies cordially. But when he locked eyes with Beale he suddenly was overwhelmed with fear, fear so pronounced that he could not utter a word, only stand and stare. It was fear of the foulest kind overwhelmed him, as Beale said, "Ah, Amir, you are a man who proclaims fealty to Mohammed, chanting that blessings and peace should be among him, but you live a life of debauchery that makes a mockery of the Koran. You are going to meet Satan soon. He is coming for you, coming for a cadre of people like you who live a lie. Opening the gates to hell will be pleasurable to admit the very foulest of mankind, of which you are one."

Amir Assad, shaking with fear, was surprised when he could swear he saw the dead Imam walk out of his house and meet Marie Laveau and walk toward Beale's home with her. Shaking almost uncontrollably by then, he excused himself and walked into The Dragon while Jasmine and Lynton were taken aback by Beale's proclamation and made no comment as Amir hurried inside. Yet, they, too, saw the dead Imam walking with Laveau. They did not mention it to Beale or Amir, but they were both shocked by what they were seeing.

Still, not intimidated by Beale, the two ladies stood their ground as Jasmine said, "My, oh my, you are a man who spews deadly verbiage with no fear of consequences."

"Ladies, I never suffer consequences. I am above and beyond that. I fear no man of this earth, and I know you were sent by a despicable man called Hercule Poirot who uses an antique phone to communicate with you. Be wise. Discard his lunatic machinations and go about the business of women. I am about the business of the grand and glorious Satan, as is my minion Marie Laveau, who accompanies me in carrying out my duties.

All the fears which these two women had grown up with, and which were now a part of their vision of the world, rose up like a wall between the world and Beale. They were facing evil like they had never seen before, and both felt ill-prepared to deal with it. And what of seeing a corpse walking about? Surely they were hallucinating.

In the meantime, the patrons at The Dragon had dispersed; and, shortly after, the proprietor, who, like a good landlord, was always last in bed, and first up, was taking, alone, his last look around the kitchen before making his final visit to the outer yard, when Amir Assad tottered into the kitchen, looking like death, his hair standing upright; as he sat down on an oak chair, all in a tremble, wiped his forehead with his hand, and, instead of speaking, heaved a great sigh or two.

Muttering with great anxiety and fear in his voice, he said, "I just dealt with the devil himself outside. We need a religious leader here, and the main one is dead. I tell you this man Beale is the devil himself. I saw the dead Imam talking to Marie Laveau and walking to Beale's house with her."

"You crazy man? A corpse can't be up walking around."

"I'm telling you what I saw."

CHAPTER 9
Face-to-Face
With the Demon of Darkness

The people wander,
Looking for sustenance,
Humming a sad song.
Thus did the Devil,
Through earth walking,
Hum low also a hellish song.

They thrive well whose garb of gore
Is Satan's choicest livery,
And they thrive well who from the poor
Have snatched the bread of penury,
And heap the houseless wanderer's store
On the rank pile of luxury.

Two Girls Who Danced
With the Demon of Darkness

The leaders thrive, though they are big;
The lawyers thrive, though they are thin;
For every gown and every wig,
Hiding the safe thrift of hell within.
And cormorants are sin-like lean,
And no compassion can be seen.

Leaving Beale, Lynton and Jasmine, with many a forlorn look right and left, and over their shoulders, went in silence perplexed. On entering the old-fashioned quadrangle, surrounded by offices, built in the antique cage work fashion, they stopped for a while under the shadow of the inn gable, and looked round the yard and listened. All was silent, nothing stirring as they watched Beale walk about the square as if he was looking for something. The lone streetlight in the square was lighted; and the proprietor of The Dragon and Amir Assad strolled about outside. He hauled Amir after him for a step or two; then stood still and shoved him for a step or two more; and thus cautiously, as a pair of skirmishers under fire, they approached the coach-house door.

The proprietor waved at the ladies and they heard him say to Amir, "There, all is safe here and no corpses are walking about. Come in and have some tea, before you go home."

"Not me, no sir. Not me. I saw that corpse walking I tell you, and that's it!" he said with a frightful shudder as he took a step backward.

"What are you afraid of? I tell you corpses don't get up and walk around. Anyway, they removed the body, so it is gone from here. You are as safe as being in a Mosque," he whispered with a nod to his companion. And at that moment a harsh laugh overhead broke the silence startlingly, and set all the dogs about barking.

"There he is," said Amir, clutching the proprietor's arm as with the other hand he pointed toward the Imam's house. "There. Looking out is window."

Overhearing the two, Lynton and Jasmine looked over at the Imam's house and sure enough, in the window of the living room, which was open; in the shadow a darker outline was visible a man, with his elbows on the window-sill, looking out at the square.

"Look at his eyes, like two live coals!" gasped Amir.

The proprietor of The Dragon could not see all this so sharply, being confused, and not so long-sighted as Amir. However, Lynton and Jasmine did see just fine and it was the Imam. They were sure of it.

While all this was occurring, Nick Beale was just leaning against an old hitching post with a smile on his face, broad and sinister. He looked at the ladies with piercing eyes. He gave them a kindly wave that accentuated his devilish smile, making it seem even more sinister. It was at this time that the proprietor motioned for the two ladies to join him and Amir.

"Wouldn't recommend you two being out here right now," the proprietor said as the two ladies came back to The Dragon. "Come back inside," he whispered fiercely motioning for them to enter. They got into the establishment, and swiftly shut the door.

"I wish we were shut of him and Beale," said Amir, with something like a groan, as he leaned against the wall of the passageway to the restaurant. "We'll sit up, and maybe wait for the dead man to come knocking on the door or maybe Beale. This is the strangest night I ever seen."

The room in The Dragon was about forty by forty square. It projected into the yard and commanded a full view of an old coach-house; and, through a narrow side window, a flanking view of the square where they could still see Nick Beale meandering about and also see the Imam's house, where the figure in the window had now disappeared.

The proprietor went into the kitchen and came out with what he called the blunderbuss, which was a twenty gauge shotgun, and loaded it with a stiff charge of bullets.

They all then sat down at the window, which was open, looking into the square, the opposite side of which was white in the brilliant moonlight. The proprietor laid the blunderbuss across his knees, and stared into the square. His comrades stared also. The door was locked; so they felt tolerably secure. Yet, it was Lynton who said, "Can that gun kill what is already dead?"

About 15 minutes passed; nothing had occurred. The clock struck one. The shadows had shifted a

Two Girls Who Danced
With the Demon of Darkness

little; but still the moon shone full on the old coach-house, and they kept looking at Beale just standing there as if he was patiently waiting for someone.

Amir thought he heard a step in the far corner. He turned but saw nothing, while Jasmine and Lynton were watching the Imam's house through the window, with eyes glazing intensely.

"Hush! Look there!" said Lynton in a whisper, as Beale moved toward the Imam's house where a towering figure dressed all in black joined him. They greeted each other with an embrace. Beale seemed in reverence to the towering black glad thing. Then the thing took on a horrific appearance. Suddenly it sprouted wings – giant flapping black wings that wrapped Beale in its embrace. The two communed in ecstasy as the creature went through a metamorphosis to become a hideous goat like entity with huge horns and grotesque fang like teeth. Then, walking down the street was Marie Laveau, who bowed in supplication before the creature.

This "thing" moved slowly toward the door of the Imam's house and the front door seemed to swing slowly open by itself as it entered, while Marie and Nick waited patiently outside. The creature returned with the dead Imam on his arm. He greeted Nick and Marie, receiving acknowledgement with a wave from Nick as he and the Imam walked into the darkness.

A thousand sparrows' wings winnowed through the air. The dogs yelled furious barks. There was a strange ring and whistle in the air. Those observing this phenomenon wondered whether it was the dead Imam's real body or just the spirit of the dead one. Nonetheless, it was obvious the "devil" had come to claim a soul, and Nick Beal and Marie Laveau were there to assist.

As a cloud crept in front of the moon, blackening the square, Nick Beal looked down at The Dragon, where four people were staring in awe at what had occurred. He gave them a big smile and motioned with a wave of his hand toward Jasmine and Lynton, indicating they should join him. Frightened, but curious, they stood up, and despite the pleas of their two male companions for them not to go, insisted on going out onto the square. They were about to once again come face-to-face with the demon of darkness.

CHAPTER 10
That Damn Phone

Why is the Father of Hell in such glee,
As he grins from ear to ear?
Why does he doff his clothes joyfully,
As he skips, prances and flaps his wings,
As he sidles, leers and twirls his stings,
And dares anyone to speak truthfully.

As Lynton and Jasmine came up to Beale and Laveau, the two of them were frightened, but determined to show no fear. They stood defiantly before them. Beale said in a determined tone, "My father always gets his souls, and this was one a long time coming. He lived a life of debauchery but tried to hide from retribution."

Two Girls Who Danced
With the Demon of Darkness

"No one can hide from retribution," stated Lynton. "It comes to us all eventually whether it is the devil getting his due or simply an act of fate."

"True my dear woman, and this Imam was prodigiously hiding his many misdeeds, and it is my dear father's sworn duty to exact payment for misdeeds. Before the so-called Imam returned here to supposedly serve humanity and lead the call to prayers, he was a paid assassin, killing many all over Northern Africa. Then he stole from the Mosque continually, as so many steal from houses of worship all over the world, while the ignorant masses foolishly funnel money into collection plates thinking they can buy their way into salvation. So you see the devil gets his due and in the process is serving mankind ever so much as does the so-called God many worship when they should be worshipping my father."

"There are probably few things we agree on," said Lynton, "but that is certainly one of them on which we can wholeheartedly agree. The masses are fools to bow before finger-pointing hypocrisy perpetrated by the leaders in houses of worship who teach more evil than good."

"Perhaps that is why that noted detective, Hercule Poirot, chose you two ladies to battle me, but many have battled me and my father and all have lost. I suggest you give up your quest, because what is coming is a retribution that will humble the entire continent. A day of reckoning is coming, and a fury is about to be unleashed like nothing that has been seen before."

Two Girls Who Danced
With the Demon of Darkness

Shocked by Beale's revelations, the two ladies bade him farewell and went back to Jasmine's place. They were awakened early the following morning by the antique phone ringing. Holding the ear piece so they could both hear, they listened attentively as Hercule Perot said, "Be prepared ladies for a most unusual situation coming your way, a situation that will help shine a light on what is going on with Nick Beale."

It was early afternoon when they heard a knock on the door, and they were surprised when two men greeted them. The two men were Saad Solomon and Sameer Maaz.

"Ladies," said Solomon "the most extraordinary and tragic affair has occurred during last night. It is the most unheard-of business. We can only regard it as a special providence that you should chance to be here at the time, for in all Morocco you are perhaps the two most qualified to deal with what happened."

Lynton and Jasmine, still a bit groggy from lack of sleep, glared at the intrusive pair with not very friendly eyes; but Lynton sat upright in the chair like an old hound that smells a very familiar scent. She waved her right hand toward the sofa, and the palpitating visitor, with his seemingly agitated companion by his side, sat upon it. Mr. Solomon was more self-contained than Mr. Maaz, but the twitching of Maaz's thin hands and the brightness of his dark eyes showed that they shared a common emotion.

"Shall I speak or you?" asked Maaz of Solomon.

Two Girls Who Danced
With the Demon of Darkness

"Well, as you seem to have made the discovery, and me to have had the information second-hand, perhaps you had better do the speaking," said Solomon.

Lynton glanced hastily at Solomon; with the more formally dressed Maaz seated beside him, and was amused at the surprise which a simple deduction had brought to Maaz's face.

Perhaps I had best say a few words first," said Solomon, "and then you can judge if you will listen to the details from Mr. Maaz, or whether we should not hasten at once to the scene of this mysterious affair. I may explain, then, that our friend here spent last evening in the company of his two brothers, Kabir and Nihal and of his sister Sabah at their house which is just up the street from a place known for its evil – the Nick Beale house."

Nodding affirmatively, Lynton said, "We know the Beale house. Go on please."

"My friend here," offered Solomon left his three siblings shortly after ten o'clock, playing cards round the dining-room table, in excellent health and spirits. This morning, being an early riser, he walked in that direction before breakfast and was overtaken by a Dr. Haider, who explained that he had just been sent for on a most urgent call to the house where his siblings lived. He naturally went with him. When he arrived at the house he found an extraordinary state of things. His two brothers and his sister were seated round the table exactly as he had left them, the cards still spread in front of them. The sister laid back stone-dead in her chair, while the two brothers sat on each side of her laughing, shouting and singing, the senses stricken clean out of them. All three of them, the dead woman and the two demented men, retained upon their faces an expression of the utmost horror, a convulsion of terror which was dreadful to look upon. There was no sign of the presence of anyone in the house, except one Noona Abeer, the old cook and housekeeper, who declared that she had slept deeply and heard no sound during the night. Nothing had been stolen or disarranged, and there is absolutely no explanation of what the horror can be which has frightened a woman to death and two strong men out of their senses."

The police have been there, but they are baffled; consequently we are following the suggestion by Mr. Poirot who called us to see you two ladies. There is the situation in a nutshell."

"Interesting indeed," offered a thoroughly perplexed Lynton.

Solomon continued, "If you can help us to clear it up you will have done a great service. You see, we got a strange call this morning from that person named Hercule Poirot, who insisted we should see you ladies."

Jasmine, having been completely quiet as she absorbed the information, said, "Glad you came to us, and we are definitely interested in exploring the situation, as it might be related to what is going on in the Beale household. Strange things are happening in the Old Quarter."

Two Girls Who Danced
With the Demon of Darkness

"We will look into this matter," Lynton said at last. "It would appear to be a case of a very exceptional nature. Have you been to the Maaz household yourself, Mr. Solomon?"

"No. Mr. Maaz brought back the account to me, and I at once hurried over with him to consult you on the matter after we received a call from Mr. Poirot, indicating we should contact you.

Jasmine said, "Then we shall walk over together. But before we start I must ask you a few questions."

Maaz had been silent all this time, but Lynton and Jasmine had observed that his more controlled excitement was even greater than the obtrusive emotion of Solomon. He sat with a pale, drawn face, his anxious gaze fixed upon Lynton, and his thin hands clasped convulsively together. His pale lips quivered as he listened to the dreadful experience which had befallen his family, and his dark eyes seemed to reflect something of the horror of the scene.

"Ask what you like," said Solomon eagerly. "It is a bad thing to speak of, but we will answer you the truth."

Looking directly at Maaz, Lynton said, "Tell me about last night, Mr. Maaz."

"Well, I supped there, as Mr. Solomon has said, and my elder brother proposed a game of Whist afterwards. We sat down about nine o'clock. It was a quarter-past ten when I moved to go. I left them all round the table, as merry as could be."

"Who let you out?" asked Jasmine.

Two Girls Who Danced
With the Demon of Darkness

"The housekeeper, Ms. Abeer, had gone to bed, so I let myself out. I shut the hall door behind me. The window of the room in which they sat was closed, but the blind was not drawn down. There was no change in door or window this morning, or any reason to think that any stranger had been to the house. Yet there they sat, driven clean mad with terror, and my sister lying dead of fright, with her head hanging over the arm of the chair. I'll never get the sight of that room out of my mind so long as I live."

"The facts, as you state them, are certainly most remarkable," said Lynton. "I take it that you have no theory yourself which can in any way account for them?"

"It's devilish, Ms. Viñas, devilish!" cried Maaz. "It is not of this world. Something has come into that room which has dashed the light of reason from their minds. What human contrivance could do that?"

"I fear," said Jasmine, "that if the matter is beyond humanity it is certainly beyond us. Yet we must exhaust all natural explanations before we fall back upon such a theory as that. As to yourself, Mr. Maaz, I take it you were divided in some way from your family, since they lived together and you had a place apart?"

"That is so, although the matter is past and done with. We were a family of hard workers who made our fortune in salt mining at Atlas Mountain, but we sold our venture to a large company, and so retired with enough to keep us. I won't deny that there was some feeling about the division of the money and it stood between us for a time, but it was all forgiven and forgotten, and we were the best of friends together."

Lynton said, "Looking back at the evening which you spent together, does anything stand out in your memory as throwing any possible light upon the tragedy? Think carefully, Mr. Maaz, for any clue which can help us."

"There is nothing at all, sir."

"Your people were in their usual spirits?" asked Jasmine.

"Never better."

"Were they nervous? Did they ever show any apprehension of coming danger?"

"Nothing of the kind."

"You have nothing to add then, which could assist us?"

Maaz considered earnestly for a moment. "There is one thing occurs to me," he said at last. "As we sat at the table my back was to the window, and my brother Nihal, he being my partner at cards, was facing it. I saw him once look hard over my shoulder, so I turned round and looked also. The blind was up and the window shut, but I could just make out the bushes on the lawn, and it seemed to me for a moment that I saw something moving among them, almost phantom like. I couldn't even say if it was man or animal, but I just thought there was something there. When I asked him what he was looking at, he told me that he had the same feeling. That is all that I can say."

Two Girls Who Danced
With the Demon of Darkness

"Did you not investigate?"

"No; the matter passed as unimportant."

"You left them, then, without any premonition of evil?"

"None at all. Of course, we had all become familiar with the tales of evil from that Beale house, but we never encountered anything to worry about from that place. We avoided it and the people who live there."

"I am not clear how you came to hear the news so early this morning," asked a very concerned Lynton.

"I am an early riser and generally take a walk before breakfast. This morning I had hardly started when the doctor overtook me. He told me that old Noona Abeer had sent a boy down with an urgent message. I sprang in beside him and we walked on. When we got there we looked into that dreadful room. They had apparently been sitting there in the dark until dawn had broken. The doctor said my sister must have been dead at least six hours. There were no signs of violence. She just lay across the arm of the chair with that look on her face. Meanwhile, my brothers were singing snatches of songs and gibbering. Oh, it was awful to see! I couldn't stand it, and the doctor was as white as a sheet. Indeed, he fell into a chair in a sort of faint, and we nearly had him on our hands as well."

"Remarkable, most remarkable!" said Lynton, rising from her chair. "I think, perhaps, we had better go to the place without further delay. I confess that I have seldom known a situation which at first sight presented a more singular problem."

The proceedings of that first morning did little to advance the investigation. It was marked, however, at the outset by an incident which left the most sinister impression upon Lynton and Jasmine. The approach to the spot at which the tragedy occurred is down a narrow, winding lane only about 100 metres from the Beale house. While they made their way along it, they heard the rattle of footsteps coming towards them and stood aside to let whoever it was pass. As the person passed them, they only caught a quick glimpse of a horribly contorted, grinning face glaring at them and smiling. Those staring eyes and gnashing teeth flashed past them like a dreadful vision. They could not make the person out, as his face was covered by a dark cloak, but the body and the eyes seemed similar to Nick Beale's. The person turned at the far corner, and like so many they had encountered disappeared from view.

As they approached the Maaz house, they were passed by a van carrying the two brothers. Maaz commented that they were probably being taken to the mental hospital. He looked with horror after the black van. Then the four of them turned their steps towards the ill-omened house in which those brothers and the sister had met their strange fate.

It was a large and bright dwelling, rather a villa than a cottage, with a considerable garden which was well filled with flowers. Towards this garden the window of the sitting-room fronted, and from it, according to Maaz, must have come that thing of evil which had by sheer horror in a single instant blasted their minds.

Lynton and Jasmine walked slowly and thoughtfully among the flower-plots and along the path before they entered the porch. So absorbed were they in their thoughts, Jasmine stumbled over the watering-pot, upset its contents, and deluged both hers and Lynton's feet and the garden path. Inside the house they were met by the elderly housekeeper, who, with the aid of a young girl who was a part-time helper, looked after the wants of the family. She readily answered all their questions. She had heard nothing in the night. Her employers had all been in excellent spirits lately, and she had never known them more cheerful and prosperous. She had fainted with horror upon entering the room in the morning and seeing that dreadful company around the table. She had, when she recovered, thrown open the window to let the morning air in, and had run down to the lane, whence she sent a neighbour for the doctor. The lady was on her bed upstairs if we cared to see her. It took four strong men to get the brothers into the asylum van. She would not herself stay in the house another day and was starting that very afternoon to rejoin her family at a place near the square in Old Town.

The police were still there and not particularly agreeable to strangers looking at the body, but let them do so anyway. It was obvious that Sabah had been a very beautiful woman, though now verging upon middle age. Her dark, clear-cut face was handsome, even in death, but there still lingered upon it something of that convulsion of horror which had been her last human emotion.

Thanking the police for allowing them to view the body, from her bedroom they descended to the sitting-room, where this strange tragedy had actually occurred. On the table were four guttered and burned-out candles that had been used for their fragrance, with the cards scattered over its surface. The chairs had been moved back against the walls, but all else was as it had been the night before. Jasmine and Lynton paced with light, swift steps about the room; they sat in the various chairs, drawing them up and reconstructing their positions. They tested how much of the garden was visible; they examined the floor, the ceiling, but never once did they see that sudden brightening of the two men's eyes and tightening of their lips which would have told them that they saw some gleam of hope.

The body was removed from the bedroom and the police left, but as the lead investigator was about to close the front door, Lynton looked over at the fireplace and asked the policemen if he had any clues why someone would have had a fire burning in the fireplace when it was not chilly out the previous night?

"Why a fire?" he said looking at Maaz "as Mr. Maaz said, there just had always been a fire in this small room on a spring evening, and it was a damp evening last night which might explain it. We are skilled investigators ma'am and believe me, we don't overlook anything."

Smiling appreciably Lynton respectfully replied, "I am sure you don't. Thank you for the information."

As the front door was slammed behind the policeman, Lynton said, "With your permission, gentlemen, we will now return to our residences, for I am not aware that any new factor is likely to come to our notice here. We will turn the facts over in our minds, and should anything occur to us we will certainly communicate with you. In the meantime I wish you both good-day."

It was not until long after they were back at Jasmine's place that Lynton broke her complete and absorbed silence. She sat coiled in an armchair, her thick black brows drawn down, her forehead contracted, her eyes vacant and far away, when she sprang to her feet.

"It won't do, Jasmine!" she said as she looked over at the abominable phone which had brought them to their current state of affairs. "Let us walk along the cobblestone streets of Old Town. We are more likely to find clues there to this problem. To let the brain work without sufficient material is like racing an engine. It racks itself to pieces. The sea air, sunshine and patience, all else will come with time.

"Now, let us calmly define our position, Jasmine," she continued as they skirted together the area around the Beale residence. "Let us get a firm grip of the very little which we do know, so that when fresh facts arise we may be ready to fit them into their places. I take it, in the first place, that neither of us is prepared to admit diabolical intrusions into the affairs of men are normal. Yet, we know the reputation of the Beale place and its proximity to the house where this latest abomination occurred. Let's begin by sensibly ruling the supernatural entirely out of our minds. There remain three persons who have been grievously stricken by some conscious or unconscious human agency. That is firm ground. Now, when did this occur? Evidently, assuming his narrative to be true, it was immediately after Maaz had left the room. That is a very important point. The presumption is that it was within a few minutes afterwards. The cards still lay upon the table. It was already past their usual hour for bed. Yet they had not changed their position or pushed back their chairs. I repeat, then, that the occurrence was immediately after his departure, and not later than eleven o'clock last night."

Nodding her head in agreement, Jasmine waited patiently for Lynton to continue, which she did. "Our next obvious step is to check, so far as we can, the movements of Maaz after he left the room. In this there is no difficulty, and the two of them seem to be above suspicion. Knowing my methods as you do not, of course, my somewhat clumsy water-pot expedient was so I could obtain a clearer impress of a footprint from whoever was outside that window than might otherwise have been possible. The wet, sandy path took it admirably. Last night was also wet with dew you will remember, and it was not difficult having obtained a sample print to pick out his track among others and to follow his movements. He appears to have walked away swiftly in the direction of the Nick Beale's house or maybe that house where the Imam lived.

"If, then, Maaz disappeared from the scene, and yet some outside person affected the card-players, how can we reconstruct that person, and how was such an impression of horror conveyed? The housekeeper may be eliminated. She is evidently harmless. Is there any evidence that someone crept up to the garden window and in some manner produced so terrific an effect that he drove those who saw it out of their senses? The only suggestion in this direction comes from Maaz himself, who says that his brother spoke about some movement in the garden. That is certainly remarkable, as the night was damp, cloudy and dark. Anyone who had the design to alarm these people would be compelled to place a very face against the glass before he could be seen. There is a three-foot flower-border outside that window, but no indication of a footmark. It is difficult to imagine, then, how an outsider could have made so terrible an impression upon the company there, nor have we found any possible motive for so strange and elaborate an attempt. You perceive our difficulties, Jasmine?"

"They are only too clear," answered Jasmine.

Two Girls Who Danced
With the Demon of Darkness

"And yet, with a little more material, we may prove that they are not insurmountable," said Lynton. "Meanwhile, we shall put the situation aside until more accurate data are available."

Lynton's power of mental detachment was a surprise to Jasmine, but sometimes she found the need to divorce herself from things in order to thoroughly access a situation. This whole trip to Casablanca had been a perplexing journey into mystery, and above all, a puzzling endeavour that was all started by that damn phone.

CHAPTER 11
Evil Afoot Here

The devil dare his whole shape uncover,
To show each feature, every limb,
Secure of an unchanging worshipper.
At this known sign, a welcome sight,
The watchful demons sought their king,
And every fiend of the dark night,
Was in an instant on the wing.

It was not until they had returned in the afternoon to Jasmine's place that they found a visitor awaiting them at the front door, who soon brought their minds back to the matter at hand. Neither of them needed to be told who that visitor was as they looked at his deerstalker hat. He was

Two Girls Who Danced
With the Demon of Darkness

puffing on a Calabash pipe. The thin body, the craggy and deeply seamed face with the fierce eyes and hawk-like nose, the grizzled hair were well-known not just in London, but all over the world. They were in the presence of the indomitable Sherlock Holmes.

© Universal Pictures

He was no surprise to them, since they had so many encounters with famous detectives. So why be surprised at the most famous one of all showing up on their doorstep. But it was a surprise to them to hear him asking in an eager voice whether they had made any advance in the reconstruction of this mysterious episode at the Maaz house. "The police are utterly at fault for not being very proactive," said he, "but perhaps your wider experience has suggested some conceivable explanation."

"Not at all," Lynton replied as Holmes took a seat since they had gone inside.

"So," offered Lynton. "Why the interest in this affair?"

"I have known of them for some time, known of their success in the salt mines." Then looking at the telephone, he continued, "Of course being told of what happened by Mr. Poirot was an added inducement that elevated my curiosity, and it was he who gave me your address."

Sensing some trepidation on Holmes's part, Lynton said, "I get the feeling that it was more than Mr. Poirot's urgings that was the motivating factor in you contacting us."

"No, I had a telegram, also."

"An old fashioned way of communicating. Might I ask from whom did you receive the telegram?" asked Lynton

A shadow passed over the gaunt face of Holmes. "You are very inquisitive," he replied.

"It is my business to be inquisitive," offered Lynton

With an effort Holmes recovered his ruffled composure. "I have no objection to telling you," he said. "It was a man named Nick Beale who sent me the telegram, saying that you two were friend's of Poirot, and that it would be advisable for me to tell you to stop your snooping."

Two Girls Who Danced
With the Demon of Darkness

"Thank you," said Lynton. "I may say that I have not cleared my mind entirely on the subject of this case, but that I have every hope of reaching some conclusion. It would be premature to say more, except that I am not one to follow the advice of someone like Mr. Beale., and I think neither are you. Perhaps you would not mind telling me if your suspicions in regards to the Maaz's point in any particular direction?"

"No, I can hardly answer that. I am in the dark in regards to this case, and am here primarily because of Poirot. Frankly, I feel that I have wasted my time and need not prolong my visit." The famous detective strode out of the home in considerable ill-humour, and as had the other detectives the two encountered, he walked away and seemed to just disappear once he got to the bottom of the steps.

Perplexed by what had occurred, the two women were surprised when a few hours later they were visited by a well-known big game hunter, a dying breed in Africa, by the name of Harvey Winner. He made it plain to them that he was interested in the case of the Maaz's, because he had encountered something unusual when on an expedition with photographers in the Atlas Mountains to locate what had been assumed was an extinct animal known as the Barbary lion. It was there the day before that he and his employers encountered a strange creature in a cave in those mountains, a creature that appeared devilish with large, flapping black wings and horns on its head.

Two Girls Who Danced
With the Demon of Darkness

It flew out of the cave, but to their surprise, left behind were an address and three names on a papyrus scroll. The names were their's and someone named Nicholas Beale, and that was why he was there. He had not been to Beale's and was leery of going there, because he had heard some very weird tales relating to Mr. Beale on previous trips to Casablanca."

"We can understand being leery of Mr. Beale, as many people are. In fact, most that are acquainted with him have very negative feelings toward him and a woman who hangs around with him named Marie Laveau."

"Marie Laveau," replied Winner. "Why do you know who Marie Laveau was?

"Was?" replied Lynton.

"Yes. Was." Offered Winner. "Marie Catherine Laveau was a Louisiana Creole practitioner of Voodoo, an herbalist and a midwife who was renowned in New Orleans. It is said she communed with the devil. She was a conjurer, who practiced Native American and African spiritualism, as well as Louisiana voodoo. She died in the 1880's."

"Well, there is someone here either using her name or she has been reincarnated and is practicing her evil in Casablanca now," replied Jasmine.

"I appreciate your information," offered Lynton.

Winner got up and excused himself, leaving with a perplexed look on his face, saying, "This has been an interesting visit."

Two Girls Who Danced
With the Demon of Darkness

"Very interesting," offered Jasmine as she showed him the door.

After he left, Lynton said to Jasmine, "There is a thread here which we had not yet grasped and which might lead us through the tangle, for I am very sure that our material has not yet all come to hand. When it does we may soon leave our difficulties behind us, because there is a definite link between Beale and what happened at the Maaz's. I am afraid there is evil afoot here."

CHAPTER 12
Reach Its Zenith in the Old Quarter

*Pale loyalty gilded a steeled brow,
With wreaths of gory laurel crowned:
The hell-hounds, Murder, Want and Woe,
Forever hungering, flocked around;
For Satan sought food,
'Twas human woe and human blood!*

Little did Lynton think how soon the words of
Holmes would be realized or how strange and
sinister would be that new development which
opened up an entirely fresh line of investigation.
She was at Jasmine's by the window in the
morning and heard the rattle of hoofs and, looking
up, she saw a dog-cart coming at a gallop down

the road. It pulled up at Jasmine's steps, and a man who was directing the dog rushed up the stairs. Lynton was already dressed, and she hastened to meet him at the door.

The visitor was so excited that he could hardly articulate, but at last in gasps and bursts his tragic story came out of him. "We are devil-ridden, ladies! The Mosque here in the square is infested with devils!" he cried. "Satan himself is loose in it! We are given over into his hands!"

He danced about in his agitation, a ludicrous object if it were not for his ashy face and startled eyes. Finally he shot out his terrible news. "Mr. Sameer Maaz died during the night, and with exactly the same symptoms as the rest of his family."

"On my," shouted Lynton as Jasmine, in shock, leaned against the wall.

Jasmine said, "We will go with you to the house."

"Of course," said the man, Hazim Hami, introducing himself.

"Hurry - hurry, before things get disarranged," shouted Lynton and they all went down the stairs and made their way to the Maaz house."

As they rushed toward the house, Jasmine and Lynton were as fast as a cheetah bounding across the plains and the man was having trouble keeping up with them.

The man was greeted at the door by the housekeeper, who had sent him to get the ladies. She was as white as a freshly laundered sheet while she struggled to put two words together. They had arrived before the doctor or the police, so that everything was absolutely undisturbed. Describing the scene exactly as it was upon that misty morning left an impression which can never be effaced from the minds of all who were there.

The atmosphere of the room where the body set in repose was of a horrible and depressing stuffiness. The housekeeper, who had first entered the room to find the body had thrown up the window, or it would have been even more intolerable. This might partly be due to the fact that an oil lamp stood flaring bright light as it sat on the table. Beside it sat the dead man, leaning back in his chair, his thin beard projecting, his spectacles pushed up on to his forehead, and his lean dark face turned towards the window and twisted into the same distortion of terror which had marked the features of his dead sister. His limbs were convulsed and his fingers contorted as though he had died in a very paroxysm of fear. He was fully clothed, though there were signs that his dressing had been done in a hurry. Those present deduced that he had spent the night there as the housekeeper had been informed by him that he was staying. Later, they would see that his bed had been slept in, and they would deduce that the tragic end had come to him in the early morning.

One could realize the red-hot energy which underlay Lynton's and Jasmine's phlegmatic exterior when one saw the sudden change which came over them from the moment that they entered the fatal house. In an instant they were tense and alert, eyes shining, faces set, limbs quivering with eager activity. They were surveying around the room, and made a quick sojourn up into the bedroom where Maaz had slept, for all the world acting like dashing foxhounds in search of prey. In the bedroom Lynton made a rapid cast around and ended by throwing open the window, which appeared to give her some fresh cause for excitement, as she leaned out of it with loud ejaculations of interest and delight. Then she rushed down the stairs with Jasmine behind her into the death room, out through the open window, threw herself upon the lawn, sprang up and into the room once more, all with the energy of the hunter who is at the very heels of quarry. The lamp, which was an ordinary standard, she examined with minute care, making certain measurements upon its bowl. She carefully scrutinized the shield which covered the top of the chimney and scraped off some ashes which adhered to its upper surface, putting some of them into an envelope she took from a desk, which she placed in her pocket. Finally, just as the doctor and the official police people put in an appearance, she beckoned to Jasmine and the housekeeper and Hami went out upon the lawn.

"I am glad to say that my investigation has not been entirely barren," Lynton remarked. "I cannot remain to discuss the matter with the police, but I should be exceedingly obliged, Mr. Hami, if you would give the inspector my compliments and direct his attention to the bedroom window and to the sitting-room lamp. Each is suggestive, and together they are almost conclusive. If the police would desire further information I shall be happy to see any of them at Jasmine's place. And now, my dear Jasmine, I think that, perhaps, we shall be better employed elsewhere."

It may be that the police resented the intrusion of an amateur or that they imagined themselves to be upon some hopeful line of investigation; but it is certain that the two ladies heard nothing from them for the entire day. During this time, Lynton and Jasmine spent some effort going over the particulars of what had been occurring there recently and conducting some experiments. One experiment served to show the line of the investigation. They had bought a lamp which was the duplicate of the one which had burned in the room where Sameer Maaz was found. It was an old fashioned oil lamp, as electricity in the Old Town was not very reliable, and it was the same oil that was used at the Mosque, and they carefully timed the period which it would take to be exhausted. Another experiment which they made was of a more unpleasant nature.

"You will remember, Jasmine," Lynton remarked in the afternoon, "that there is a single common point of resemblance in the varying reports which have reached us. This concerns the effect of the atmosphere of the room in each case upon those who had first entered it. You will recollect that Maaz, in describing the episode of his last visit to his brother's house, remarked that the elderly doctor on entering the room fell into a chair? Now, you will remember also that the housekeeper told us that she herself got dizzy upon entering the room and had afterwards opened the window. In the second case in regards to Maaz you cannot have forgotten the horrible stuffiness of the room when we arrived, though the housekeeper had thrown open the window. That housekeeper, I found upon inquiry, was so ill that she had gone to her bed. You will admit, Jasmine, that these facts are very suggestive. In each case there is evidence of a poisonous atmosphere. In each case, also, there is combustion going on in the room--in the one case a fire, in the other a lamp. The fire was needed, but the lamp was still lit as a comparison of the oil consumed will show, long after it was broad daylight. Why? Surely because there is some connection between three things, the burning, the stuffy atmosphere, and, finally, the madness or death of those unfortunate people. That is clear, is it not?"

"It would appear so."

"At least we may accept it as a working hypothesis. We will suppose, then, that something was burned in each case which produced an atmosphere causing strange toxic effects. Very good. In the first instance, that of the Maaz family, minus Sameer of course, this substance was placed in the fire. Now the window was shut, but the fire would naturally carry fumes to some extent up the chimney. Hence one would expect the effects of the poison to be less than in the second case, where there was less escape for the vapour. The result seems to indicate that it was so, since in the first case only the woman, who had presumably the more sensitive organism, was killed, the others exhibiting that temporary or permanent lunacy which is evidently the first effect of the drug. In the second case the result was complete. The facts, therefore, seem to bear out the theory of a poison which worked by combustion. With this train of reasoning in my head, I naturally looked about in Maaz's room to find some remains of this substance. The obvious place to look was the talc shelf or smoke-guard of the lamp. There, sure enough, I perceived a number of flaky ashes and round the edges a fringe of brownish powder, which had not yet been consumed. Half of this I took, as you saw, and I placed it in an envelope."

"Why half, Lynton?"

"It is not for me, my dear Jasmine, to stand in the way of the official police force. I leave them all the evidence which I found. The poison still remained so they might find it. Now Jasmine, we will light our lamp; we will, however, take the precaution to open our window to avoid the premature decease of two deserving members of society, and you will seat yourself near that open window in an armchair unless, like a sensible person, you determine to have nothing to do with the affair. This chair I will place opposite yours, so that we may be the same distance from the poison and face to face. The door we will leave ajar. Each is now in a position to watch the other and to bring the experiment to an end should the symptoms seem alarming. Is that all clear? Well, then, I take the powder I found and put in the envelope, what remains of it, and I lay it above the burning lamp. So! Now Jasmine let us sit down and await developments."

They were not long in coming. Lynton had hardly settled into her chair before she was conscious of a thick, musky odour, subtle and nauseous. At the very first whiff of it her brain and Jasmine's imagination were beyond all control. A thick, black cloud swirled before their eyes, and their minds told them that in this cloud, unseen as yet, but about to spring out upon their appalled senses, lurked all that was vaguely horrible, all that was monstrous and inconceivably wicked in the universe. Vague shapes swirled and swam amid the dark cloud-bank, each a menace and a warning of something coming, the advent of some unspeakable dweller upon the threshold, whose very shadow would blast souls. A freezing horror took possession of them. They felt that their hair was rising, that their eyes were protruding, that their mouths were opened, and their tongues were like leather. The turmoil within their brains was such that something snapped. They tried to scream and were vaguely aware of some hoarse croak which was their own voices, but distant and detached. At the same moment, in some effort of escape, Lynton broke through that cloud of despair and had a glimpse of Jasmine's face, white, rigid, and drawn with horror, the very look which Lynton had seen upon the features of the dead people in the Maaz house. It was a vision which gave her an instant of sanity and strength. She dashed from her chair, threw her arms around Jasmine, and together they lurched through the door, and threw themselves down upon the porch and were lying side by side, conscious only of the glorious sunshine which was bursting its way through the hellish cloud of terror which had consumed them. Slowly it rose from their souls like the mists from a landscape of lost hope until peace and reason had returned, and they were sitting upon the porch, wiping their clammy foreheads, and looking with apprehension at each other to mark the last traces of that terrifying experience which they had undergone.

"Upon my word, Jasmine!" said Lynton at last with an unsteady voice, "I owe you both my thanks and an apology. It was an unjustifiable experiment even for one's self, and doubly so for a friend. I am really very sorry."

"You know," Jasmine answered with some emotion, "that it is my greatest joy and privilege to be assisting such an astute individual."

Lynton lapsed at once into the half-humorous, half-cynical vein. "It would be superfluous to drive us mad, my dear girl," said she. "A candid observer would certainly declare that we were so already mad before we embarked upon so wild an experiment. I confess that I never imagined that the effect could be so sudden and so severe."

Two Girls Who Danced
With the Demon of Darkness

Lynton dashed into the cottage, holding her breath and doused the lamp. "We must give the room a little time to clear. I take it Jasmine that you have no longer a shadow of a doubt as to how these tragedies were produced?"

"None whatever."

With a look of deep concern, Lynton said, "But the cause remains as obscure as before. I think we must admit that all the evidence points to something more brutal here than just the supernatural. There is an evil lurking about that is far more sinister than the mere supernatural, and it is about to reach its zenith in the Old Quarter.

CHAPTER 13
I Guess I am Doomed

Hark! The earthquake's crash I hear,
Kings turn pale and conquerors fear to start,
Ruffians tremble with fear,
For Satan from his liar doth depart.

This man, Sameer Maaz, was the victim in the second tragedy, but this tragedy and the previous one cannot be divorced from the bitter familial quarrel that had led to acrimony among the individuals and, at the time, Lynton and Jasmine could not effectively ascertain how hollow the reconciliation might have been. When evaluating Sameer Maaz, with the foxy face and the small shrewd, beady eyes behind his spectacles, he was not a man who would be judged to be of a particularly forgiving disposition. Yet, his death was one that lent another element of mystery to what had truly happened and why.

For that reason, Lynton said to Jasmine, "There was someone moving in the garden, which took attention for a moment from the real cause of the tragedy. Finally, if Maaz did not throw the substance into the fire at the moment of leaving the room, who did do so? The affair happened immediately after his departure. Had anyone else come in, the family would certainly have risen from the table. Besides, common decency among people precluded individuals from arriving to visit that late at night. It might then be taken that all the evidence points to Sameer Maaz as the culprit."

"Then could his own death be suicide, as a result of remorse?" asked Jasmine.

"Well, it is on the face of it a not impossible supposition. The man who had the guilt upon his soul of having brought such a fate upon his own family might well be driven by remorse to inflict retribution upon himself. There are, however, some cogent reasons against it. Fortunately, there is one man who knows all about it, and that is none other than Mr. Nicholas Beale."

As the police investigated and listened irreverently later to Lynton's theories, they were too centred on their own presumed infallibilities to give any real credence to what the two ladies had postulated, but Lynton, and Jasmine in support of her, proposed a solution to the situation which

Two Girls Who Danced
With the Demon of Darkness

drew upon what had happened recently with the death of the Imam. They shared the information in regards to the apparent appearance of someone or some thing outside that window the night of the Maaz woman's death. They did not, however, mention Nick Beale, as they assumed any reference to the supernatural, of which he was a representative, would be scoffed at by the police.

When they got back to Jasmine's place, there was Nick Beale waiting at the door. He presented, at that particular time, a majestically grand figure of manhood, but with a dark nature about him that instilled fear. He turned toward them with eyes blazing daggers.

"I think you want to see me, ladies. I have come, though I really do not know why I should be here, except that I have great respect for the two of you."

Motioning for him to come inside as she opened the door, Jasmine said, "Perhaps we can clear a point up that intrigues us. Meanwhile, we are much obliged to you for your courteous presence, and much appreciative of your respect for us. You will excuse this informal reception, but my friend Lynton and I have nearly furnished an additional chapter to what the people of the Old Quarter have often called the *Beale Terror*. We prefer a clear atmosphere for the present. Perhaps, since the matters which we have to discuss will affect you personally in a very intimate fashion, it is as well that we should talk here, free of the police, where there can be no eavesdropping"

Two Girls Who Danced
With the Demon of Darkness

"I am at a loss to know," he said, "what you can have to speak about which affects me personally in a very intimate fashion."

"The killing of the Maaz woman and her brother and the apparent insanity of the other two brothers," said Lynton.

For a moment Lynton wished that she was armed. Then again, what could be accomplished with armaments when dealing with this level of evil

Beale's fierce face turned to a dusky red, his eyes glared, and the knotted, passionate veins pulsated out in his forehead, while with clenched hands he seemed to be contemplating violence. Then with a supreme effort he resumed a cold, rigid calmness, which was, perhaps, more suggestive of danger than a typical hot-headed outburst.

"I have got into the way of being a law to myself. You would do well, ladies, not to forget it, for I have no desire to do you an injury, at least not right now."

"Nor do we have any desire to do you an injury. Surely the clearest proof of it is that, knowing what we know, I am talking to you and not to the police."

Beale sat down with a gasp, overawed for, perhaps, the first time in his adventurous life. There was a calm assurance of power in Lynton's manner and that of Jasmine as well. Beale stammered for a moment his hands opening and shutting in his agitation.

Two Girls Who Danced
With the Demon of Darkness

"What do you mean?" he asked at last. "If this is bluff upon your part, ladies, you have chosen a bad man for your experiment. Let us have no more beating about the bush. What do you mean?"

"I will tell you," said Lynton, "and the reason why I tell you is that I hope frankness may beget frankness. What my next step may be will depend entirely upon the nature of your own defence."

"My defence?"

"Yes, sir."

"My defence against what?"

"Against the charge of killing the Imam, Ms. Maaz and Mr. Maaz."

For the first time, there was an element of fright about Beale as he mopped his forehead with his handkerchief. "Upon my word, you are getting on my nerves," said he. "Do all your successes depend upon this prodigious power of bluff?"

"The bluff," said Lynton sternly, "is upon your side and not upon mine. As a proof I will tell you some of the facts upon which my conclusions are based. First, I know you were one of the factors which had to be taken into account in reconstructing the drama hereabouts for many years. You love playing the role of a demon, and I am convinced you have formed a coven of evil-loving people to promulgate fear in individuals hereabouts."

Smiling, he said, "Really?"

"I have analyzed your reasons and regard them as unconvincing and inadequate. We will pass that. You are curious, which is why you came here. I suspect you in the murders. You have been friends with the Imam for years is my guess, and then went to his house after we visited with him."

"How do you know that?"

"Simple deduction. As Sherlock Holmes would say, elementary my dear Watson. When prompted by," she then looked at the telephone, "that telephone to check on you, we were aghast what we found, but you loved playing the game. You get great enjoyment out of being a so-called demon. It gives you a feeling of great power over people."

"You are an astute observer."

"I am, indeed. That is what you may count on when I investigate you. You spent a restless night at your place last night for example, as I can see by your discombobulated look and extremely tired eyes. You, no doubt, formed certain plans, which in the early morning you proceeded to put into execution. Leaving your house, probably just as day was breaking, you filled your pocket with some reddish gravel that was lying heaped beside your gate, which I observed when visiting your home."

Beale gave out a sigh and looked at Lynton in amazement as she continued her baiting of him. "You then walked swiftly to the Imam's house would be my guess. You were wearing, I may remark, the same pair of ribbed tennis shoes which are at the present moment are upon your feet. At the Imam's, you passed through the orchard and the side hedge, based upon what I see on your tennis shoes. It was now daylight. You drew some of the gravel from your pocket, and you threw it up at the window above you."

"Amazing," offered Beale.

"Thank you. I agree. Sometimes I am indeed amazing. Sometimes I even amaze myself; consequently, I will continue."

Beale sprang to his feet. "I believe that you are the real devil here!" he cried.

Lynton smiled at what she considered a compliment. "It took two, or possibly three, handfuls of stones before the person came to the window. I say that, because I can see by lack of bulging in your coat pocket that most of the stones are gone."

He sat back down with a look of astonishment on his face. He leaned back in his chair, as if he was actually enjoying having his crimes analyzed by a superb mastermind of detection.

"Now, as to why you were there at the Imam's home. You see, I investigated the Imam, and I know it was not he who died, but someone who looked a lot like him. I am not an expert on the Muslim religion, but I do know that while generally discouraged, autopsies are permitted in Islam under certain circumstances, particularly when they are deemed necessary for legal or medical reasons. The Islamic principle of public benefit, referred to as *maslaha* can justify an autopsy if it serves a greater good, like determining the cause of death in a criminal investigation or advancing some type of medical knowledge. However, it's important to minimize delay in burial and to perform the autopsy with utmost respect for the deceased. Now, this trait was utilized in the Imam's case, and no autopsy was performed, as I checked to see. So, when the Imam was seen after his death, he was not a ghost, but the real Imam. You and your cohorts were smuggling him out of the city, because you were afraid the truth of his escape from a prison in Algeria would be discovered. Now, it appears his sojourn in prison was for nothing too serious; consequently, I am not here to judge him for his crimes. I do know that a man can rob a convenience store for food to feed his family and get 20 years in prison, while the banker who steals millions from people only gets a slap on the wrist. This is the system of justice in a world where the rich and powerful always get a pass, while the poor are escorted to the slammer. I found it out about the Imam through exhaustive personal research. Also, once he was assumed dead, there was no need for more investigation. My guess is that you obtained an unclaimed corpse from the morgue and substituted it for the Imam. The boarder was in on the switch, but now to why you needed to see the boarder."

Squirming in his seat, Beale was mesmerized by the fact Lynton had been so thorough in uncovering the plot. He bowed his head and said, "So continue please. I am fascinated."

"So, you beckoned his boarder to come down. You probably entered by the window to avoid being seen. You were discussing how the Imam was spirited away so no one would see him. Now, how you managed the apparent fake demons appearing at various venues and times is beyond me at present."

"How do you know they were fake?"

"I don't, but I don't really care at this point. My guess is you have now spirited the boarder out of town also to avoid discovery. However, I am more concerned with the fake death of the Imam and the murder of two people at the Maaz residence, which is at your doorstep. My guess is those are only a couple of the sinister deeds you have promulgated, as people have been disappearing around here for years with no credible explanation.

"You really think the police will accept this fantastic yarn?" asked Beale.

"Probably not, unfortunately." Replied Lynton. "But for your edification, I will tell you how the murders were masterfully carried out. You never killed anyone in regards to the Imam's corpse. That was just a well-timed and well-coordinated replacement corpse that you masterfully substituted so he would be assumed to have been killed.

Beale was smiling, despite his elaborate plan being deduced by Lynton and Jasmine. Lynton continued. "Now, the deaths and brain damage to the Maaz's was a bit more complex. First, one would want to know why they had to be killed, which is easily explained by checking the history of the two families. You were all, according to corporate records I researched, partners in the salt mines at Atlas Mountain. Your grandfather was partners with them, and he was bamboozled out of millions when they arranged to kill him, using the same method you used on them. They put cyanide powder in oil lamps is my guess. That did away with your grandfather, but it took you years to figure it out, because you were just a small boy when he died. All those years you masterfully plotted revenge, playing your role as a demon much to your delight, and you were working with the Imam to institute it when things got too hot for him in the Old Quarter and you decided it was best to get him out of here. Fortunately, you had the help of your friend, Marie Laveau, who loved playing the role of a former voodoo queen.

You were the one that Sameer Maaz's brother saw outside that fateful night. You had put cyanide powder in the lamp and in the fireplace. You intended to kill all four of them, but Sameer Maaz left early, before it had time to take effect. Then, he came back and you slipped in and poured powder in the lamp again, and it was most effective the second time. Our visitor's face had turned ashen Their visitor's face turned grey as he listened to the words of his accuser. Now he sat for some time in thought with his face sunk in his hands, his mode of superiority totally crushed. Then with a sudden impulsive gesture he plucked a photograph from his breast-pocket and tossed it on the table.

Two Girls Who Danced
With the Demon of Darkness

"Good, but far from perfect I am afraid. That is the real reason I have done it," said he.

It was a picture showing the bust and face of a very beautiful woman. Lynton and Jasmine examined it. Lynton said, "A woman you loved, but you, for reasons of propriety had, at a young age, married Ms. Maaz, and you were stuck with her, because she would not agree to a divorce, and neither of you are Muslim. You were both Catholic in a very traditional country whether Muslim or Christian.

"Yes, that was one way they kept me quiet about the whole affair. For years I have loved her. For years she has loved me. There is the secret of that seclusion which people have marvelled at. It has brought me close to the one thing on earth that was dear to me. I could not marry her, for I have a wife who because of deplorable laws, I could not divorce. For years that wonderful woman waited. For years I waited. And these deaths are what we have waited for." A terrible sob shook his great frame, and he clutched his throat under his brindled beard. Then with an effort he mastered himself and spoke on. "The Imam knew. He was in our confidence. He would tell you that she was an angel upon earth. There you have the missing clue to my action, ladies."

He then drew from his pocket a paper packet and laid it upon the table. On the outside was written *Radix pedis diaboli* with a red poison label beneath it. He pushed it towards the girls. "That is what I used, basically it is cyanide."

Two Girls Who Danced
With the Demon of Darkness

"Devil's-foot root! I know the concoction, yes." Offered Lynton.

"The root is shaped like a foot, half human, half goat=like; hence the fanciful name given by laymen. It is used as an ordeal poison by the medicine-men in certain districts of West Africa and is kept as a secret among them. This particular specimen I obtained under very extraordinary circumstances in the Ubangi country."

He opened the paper as he spoke and disclosed a heap of reddish-brown, snuff-like powder. "Much more effective than cyanide and much more untraceable. I am so impressed with you ladies figuring this out. I guess I am doomed."

**Two Girls Who Danced
With the Demon of Darkness**

EPILOGUE
Nick Beale Had Just Found That Out

This day fiends give to revelry
To celebrate their king's return,
And with delight its sire to see
Hell's adamantine limits burn.

But were the Devil's sight is keen
As reason's penetrating eye,
His sulphurous majesty wean,
Would find but little cause for joy.

For the sons of reason see
That, ere fate consume the pole,
The false tyrant's cheek shall be
Bloodless as his coward soul.

J. Wayne Frye

Two Girls Who Danced
With the Demon of Darkness

"I suppose you want me to go to the police with you and confess," said a dejected Beale.

"Why?" replied Lynton. "You think any of this is genuinely provable in a court of law? Your soul cried out for revenge. You have spent much of your life developing a devilish persona, but that alone could not convict you. Maybe its time for you to cast that persona aside and join the community of men. I have loved a man as you have loved a woman, so I can understand your feelings. My father-in-law once said, 'Some people need killing, but who has the nerve to do it.' I am not judging whether you are right or wrong, but I can understand your reasons for doing what you did. I might act even as you have. Who knows? And now my dear Mr. Beale, I think we may dismiss the matter from our minds."

These two ladies who had danced with the demon of darkness represented a rare breed. They kept their word. They gave it their all. They put themselves last for those they cared about. These individuals rarely received the same compassion and effort in return, yet continued to give freely. They were the givers, forgivers and selfless individuals who kept pushing forward no matter what barriers were placed before them. They were the ones who always stood by you in times of turmoil. They never lost the part of them which showed beauty in small things. They refused to be broken by conventionality no matter how harsh the world might seem. They believed there was good in people. They refused to let the bad keep them from seeing good. They refused to lose the courage to be open-minded, to show kindness even when it is sometimes not returned. They believed that every kind word, every small act of love left something good behind and nothing kind was ever wasted. They chose to be gentle, kind and full of love even when it was hard. They knew they lived in a cruel world, but they had room for kindness and love. They knew hope still flickered in the darkest moments and that softness could survive, even in the hardest of times. Nick Beale had just found that out.